as rivers flow

JOHN SAUL was born in Liverpool and now lives in Suffolk. After study-ing philosophy and politics at Oxford and French language and litera-ture in Paris he lived and worked in London, Vancouver, Guayaquil and Hamburg, where he has been the translator for the German section of Greenpeace. He is the author of the novel, *Finistère*, forthcoming from Salt, and two further collections of stories, *Call It Tender* and *The Most Serene Republic: love stories from cities.*

john saul

as rivers flow

SALT

CAMBRIDGE

PUBLISHED BY SALT PUBLISHING
14a High Street, Fulbourn, Cambridge CB21 5DH United Kingdom

First published 2009

Printed in Great Britain by the MPG Books Group, Bodmin and King's Lynn

Typeset in Swift 11 / 14

ISBN 978 1 84471 575 6 paperback

Salt Publishing Ltd gratefully acknowledges
the financial assistance of Arts Council England

1 3 5 7 9 8 6 4 2

CONTENTS

MERSEY

L ET THOSE LIGHTS go on. Let: my favourite word from
the beginning: let. It speaks authority. Let the party
begin. Let the dust settle.

After seventy years it has. Here I am coming down Dale
Street into Queensway, looking down the mouth of the old
Mersey Tunnel. In 1934 the biggest road tunnel in the
world. Who then said: Let the lights be switched on—? It
was bearded King George V of England.

At the end of North John Street, notepad in hand, my
future dad, tall, blue eyes, straw-coloured teeth, was
standing listening. Simmering still from a row with his
editor at the *Daily Post*. My mum with her mum. 200,000
people including entire schools who had trekked into
town from all over, Allerton, Huyton, Toxteth, Bootle and
Anfield, down Mount Pleasant and Scotland Road, in the
heat that followed the cloudbursts in the night.

The union jacks waved, the green and gold curtains
drew back, jerkily, pulled by strong arms because the gold
switch pushed by the King failed to start the motors; the
strong arms pulled their strongest because 200,000 people,
a crowd rippling with the emotions of expectations, can't
give up their day not to see a tunnel mouth. They have to
be able to salute the engineering which drilled the two
pilot bore-holes to within one inch of each other, which
saw the roof defy the very Mersey by just four feet of rock.
They must have their aspirations as humans reflected in
the perfection of the broad bends of roadway, divinely lit;

the sight of the tunnel mouth is their due as citizens, even if some, like my mum's mum, had been content enough to see Queen Mary's dress and hat, or stare at the raindrops on the teakwood and cream enamel of the royal train stopped in Lime Street.

My dad felt his own switch thrown. Glory be, someone in the crowd called when the tunnel mouth appeared in all its lights, green and gold and warm just as my mum's mum could have hoped for. The tiles were exactly the right cream. May, my grandmother said to my mother, remember that colour. That cream on the walls is just the colour I want for the living room. What? said May, who had just noticed my dad—not of course with a label stuck to his forehead saying dad, or husband—but getting purple over this shout of Glory be.

Are you all right? May said to him.

What?

That was his first word to my future mother. My mother. His greeting: What?

You look, well, you don't look ill exactly, but you're not enjoying yourself.

Enjoying myself?

He glared. Angry that this could be a possible description of his state. Enjoying yourself is what moon men might do. Rabbits. Girls with dolls' houses. Fred Astaire.

I've got trouble at work, he said. Now there'll be more.

Come on dear, said May's mother, we shall see better from up the steps. I want to see for myself if his trousers are creased at the sides, as they say, not at the front and the back.

Oh no, said May. Not these steps, my dress won't like it.

It could be your last chance, said my future dad prophetically. That man'll be dead in two years.

2

We must go down the tunnel soon, mother, said May. Father will take us. He said so. We didn't go to the peek previews and now we will be going in style.

Have you noted down the opening hours, dear? said my grandmother.

Just daylight hours—at first, my father informed them. The next thing we know there'll be operators at the booths at all hours, at Christmas even. But is my paper going to say that?

Paper? said my grandmother.

I work at the *Daily Post*.

Look, said May, he's giving those children medals.

They'll be commemorative, my grandmother commented. You won't be wanting one?

I'm 24 years old, mother.

Blushing, she looked at my father, who was scribbling hectically on his notepad. My mother watched but didn't want to interrupt. His absorption with his notebook, his blue eyes fixed there, let her do as she liked. She daydreamed. His hair was fair and neatly parted and wavy, like hair sometimes was in the cartoons. He wrote frantically no matter how jostled he was by the crowd, no matter how much she looked at him and loosed her guesses. What could he dance? Maybe he played tennis, cricket? Or maybe a newshawk had no spare time? He would definitely be too busy writing up events in London and America. About Bonny and Clyde (maybe he knows why the car they died in had a half-eaten sandwich and a saxophone inside?), about the revolution in Mexico. China. Oh what a whirlwind the world was in, what a giddy maelstrom. Look at all these people. Those people on the rooftop there. And there, clinging to the chimneys. What a calamity if they fell. And see that woman in the white suit with that priceless necktie, trying to be Marlene Dietrich.

My father was pushed up so close she could almost read his writing. He licked his pencil and flipped to a new page, all in a trice. She guessed he had one jacket and this was that jacket. Those wide lapels. She daydreamed he'd been admitted to her hospital. She tried to guess how he would behave if he was a patient sitting up looking at her with his blue eyes and wavy hair. She wondered if someone had invented a scale of dark hair and blondness and where exactly his fair hair would reach on the scale. Was blondness so special and what difference could it make? He dashed on to the next page. His pencil was a stub. What would take him to the hospital in the first place, would it be a wrist sprained from over-reporting?

Glory, he said in disgust—glory. Seventeen men died building this tunnel.

Are you speaking to me? said May.

He looked her way for the first time and immediately his expression changed. At her comely looks, said to resemble Gracie Fields, at her smile as it followed her frown.

I wasn't, he said with a stutter, but I suppose I am now.

So? she said provocatively. Seventeen men died, but you can't build a tunnel such as this, in which streams of wheeled traffic may run in light and safety—you heard the King, you wrote it down I expect.

Light and safety, yes, my father read. Below the depths and turbulence of tidal water bearing ships of the world. Many hundreds have toiled here, etcetera, etcetera, struggled—

For long months against mud and darkness to bring it into being.

Being, yes. May our peoples—

4

May, that's my name.

What?

It comes up sometimes, just like that.

I was going to say: how can you remember so much of his speech, you aren't writing it down like I am.

I just can.

She's always been particularly good at that, my grandmother leant across to add. Mind you, if you speak to people like he does, well, bless his great beard. But what is upsetting you so?

Well. Seventeen men died and what does our King George say about this? Nothing. It's a disgrace. Now I'm going back to the paper and I will say to my editor, we must print this. We should say: King George made no mention of the fact seventeen workers died.

What for?

What *for*?

Mother leave him alone. It's his work. I think it's right he should say this if it's true.

Of course it's true. Even King George knows it's true.

Then it is true, said my mother's mother.

I must get back to the office, my father said. Let—

Yes—

May, you have the poor man stuck for words. And a newshawk. It's your hat.

This old hat?

Well all right. It's your dress.

It's only an afternoon dress, mother.

It was one of the best at Marshall and Snelgrove's.

It was not. We found this at Broadbent's.

Look now, May, they're driving through the arch with those ocean liners in stone above them. I do believe he's going to Birkenhead.

5

I was going to say, said my father, perhaps we could meet for a cup of tea in an hour or so? I know a fine place just by the Tatler.

Tatler?

That new news theatre. It'll be jam packed of course. All these people looking for somewhere to go, out of the sizzling sun.

Well, said my grandmother. I'm going to surprise you. I'm going to leave you here, May, I'm going to go down to the tunnel and look at those lights. Your father will have listened to His Majesty on the radio and he will want to know so many details.

This thoroughfare is great and strange, said May repeating the words of the King. The wonder of your tunnel will only come into mind after reflection.

It will dear. I want to look more closely at those cream tiles. Those lights are beautiful.

They're embedded, said my father.

Embedded? said my mother reddening.

That's why they look so fine. And they are lit by two separate power stations, alternately. One light is lit by one station, the next by the other station, the next by the first station and so on. When there's a power cut half the lights will stay on.

That's so clever. Isn't that clever, mother? Mother?

She's gone.

She would have crossed the bottom of Dale Street, moving down the crowd towards the toll booths.

Mother? called May on tiptoe.

She can't hear. Why not just let her go.

It feels strange, said May. Like everything has stopped for a moment. Even the Mersey.

It hasn't, my dad contradicted. The river flows always.

6

What?
Let him say this to her. Let her let him say this.

ELBE

TWO BLACK TUGS begin turning a container vessel in the grey waters of the Elbe. This is the *Hanjin Taipei*, broader and longer than the *Titanic*. The white letters of HANJIN, thirty feet tall, the tail of the J dropping below the others, stand confidently on its black-painted side. Its containers, in workmanlike blue, dark green and rust likewise carry the company name and its circular yin-yang logo.

Walking her hunched-shouldered walk down the office corridor Victoria sees the black hull filling the end-window, cutting out the sky and dimming the daylight as the *Taipei* moves across. Nonetheless she walks straight to her office. To the piles of papers and the computer screen, the Black-Berry lying on a table next to her mobile phone. All of which she uncharacteristically ignores. From her own window, the black wall of steel has become more recognisably a ship arriving on the tide. The moment she goes to the window a cable to the tug below, the *Accurat*, draws taut. A second tug busies itself into position at the heel of the giant, readying itself to turn the *Hanjin Taipei* in a circle.

Dear Victoria, she reads again in the note Paul sent. *On or around the 24th—we always say on or around—we should arrive in your town although we will dock for a few hours only. Why not meet me? Call the Schiffsmeldedienst in Finkenwerder (www.smd.de). They will be able to say exactly when we come in. Then give me a call. I have something for you from Los Angeles and you can bring me one of those boxes of marzipan. If you want. It would be lovely just to see you after all these years.*

Bemused that for the second time that day she should

stop and watch a ship instead of dealing with urgent decisions, Victoria stays by the window. Sniffing, feeling a cold
or worse coming on, she looks across the river at the blue
peachy light, a yellow haze behind the container port and
above the horizon, the Harburg hills, behind everything
like a wash. Down the river, to her right, clouds in a line
over the far bank stretch into the distance, over the termi-
nals and the oil storage tanks, to where the whole sky is
dark and the last cranes mere silhouettes in the darkness.
Below her, pitching and striving, a flat blue *barkasse* barge
scurries to avoid the great bows before they squeeze out the
space for its passage.

From the pontoon restaurant Deborah and Merryweather
—that surname he always got called by—watched the
Hanjin container ship pass under a darkening sky on its
way up the Elbe. They kept watching until it was behind
her and only he had it in sight. All that expansive water,
began Deborah pretending to shiver with fear at the
thought. Expensive water? said Merryweather. Ex*pan*sive,
said Deborah; that water is so close it could swallow us any
moment. But we're floating, said Merryweather. How true,
replied Deborah, like jellyfish. Logs, said Merryweather
looking past her shoulder. She glanced round to see what
he was looking at. The receding ship was slowly changing
shape to start turning broadside on. Do you remember that
song, 'Little Boxes', when we were students? he asked her
(they were trying hard to reconnect after years in different
places). Deborah, having filled the seat beside her with her
coat, bags, phone, beret, camera and pocket dictionary, was
looking with delight at her fish soup which had come in a
glass jar with a clasp. This is exotic, a *compote* jar, she said,
is that the word? Well actually I was talking about *boxes*,

9

said Merryweather, not jars, and those containers are *big boxes*. I suppose so, said Deborah, just look at that yellow thing, is it a pepper? Ooh, and that's a to*mato*. I'm going to *photo*graph this. Did you hear what I said? said Merryweather. I did, said Deborah, but you seem to be taking a long time to get to the point; are you going to make a hit record with a song called 'Big Boxes', are you going to go straight to the studio or what? Well no, said Merryweather, what do you mean, *studio*? *I* don't know, said Deborah, you called me up out of the blue because you had this meeting here and you knew I was passing through, how in God's— how did you know I was even here, have you got spies out because if you have you'd better recall them quick, and oh dear now I've flustered you, I should have just asked you questions outright and what do I do, I fluster people, I don't mean to create harm, havoc. But sometimes people just get tangled in my propeller. That was rather a clever thing to say, don't you think, Merry, given that we were talking about ships? Deborah, said Merryweather, please relax; I was just drawing your attention to the fact that that ship out there was full of big boxes and nowadays everything is in packages and that's all we care about. This soup isn't a package, Deborah objected. You know what I mean. I don't, said Deborah; all *who* cares about? *Alles in Ordnung?* asked the waiter. Ya, yes, *Danke*, said Merryweather. *Ja*, said Deborah looking down at and then up from her dictionary. She smiled hugely at the waiter, as if he had handed her the very present she wanted for her birthday. *Meiner Herr, die Suppe ist köstlich.* Wait wait, Deborah said to him, because I *do* like these yellow tulips you've put on the table. *Und die Tulpen sind—fabelhaft.* The waiter returned the compliments by raising his eyebrows but in a way that was approving. And I see you, der Herr, the waiter said, are pointing to the ship just now, well any moment there will come a few waves, yes. Rolling. Just a little. A few. There, you see. I see, whoa, said Merryweather swaying at the table, exaggerating the pontoon's movement. There it is still, he said. Where's what still? said Deborah. That ship, it looks like it's turning round. Turning round? said Deborah, why?

The little *barkasse* hoots to the *Accurat* as it edges by. Every ten years (she has been here twenty) a *barkasse* has a collision and sinks. With her eyes fixed on the great ship, Victoria stretches both arms towards the ceiling; pushes up one arm, then the other, so her shoulders feel the exercise. She does this ten times. The *Hanjin Taipei* turns and turns. Its length shortens and its great body begins to taper. The bows grow as they move closer to the office building. In a scrape with this steel colossus, thinks Victoria, these walls would crumble like old cake. But such manoeuvres are routine. The *QE2* regularly passes this way, and any day now there'll be the *Queen Victoria. Victoria*: in his next note Paul would be sure to mention the new Queen ship. But there was no way she was going to the terminal to meet him, any more than she had gone to the dozens of rendezvous he had suggested over the years. She wondered if she should have his notes sent back to him, have his hopes of meeting her become more realistic, destroy these hopes altogether.

Anything could be in those boxes, said Merryweather trying a spoonful of Deborah's soup. Looking up, he was distracted by a message ticking across a screen above the restaurant counter. Deborah turned round to see what he saw. I can't decipher that, can you? Something about ships, said Merryweather. You were saying, said Deborah. I was saying anything could be in those boxes; it's all hidden nowadays;

everything undesirable is hidden. Do you think I'm undesirable? said Deborah suddenly. I—erm, later, said Merryweather blushing, right now I mean things like pollution, the sorts of things your half-sister's organisation deals with. I don't say 'half-sister', Deborah corrected, I say sister. Sister, said Merryweather, now let me finish my point—you don't see CO_2. You can't recognise a terrorist by looking. I know, said Deborah, like genetic engineering; this fish could have been genetically engineered and I wouldn't taste it. Are you sure about that? said Merryweather. Not sure, no, said Deborah standing and holding her camera over the soup; so what *is* in boxes like that, bananas, computers? Anything, said Merryweather: tractors, stowaways, households. A flash lit the restaurant as Deborah clicked the shutter. What do you mean, households?

The cables are on, we're turning. I have nothing to do except hope Victoria makes it to the ship. No tasks. I can be on the bridge and look through the binoculars from up high. There are the churches, there the almost interminable dockland. Hills and woods to the south. Astonishing how many people I see are watching us. Along the banks, in the windows of houses and restaurants and offices. They see we are somehow mighty but don't know what to make of us. Don't know where we have been or what it's like for us. They see us arriving and leaving, entering estuaries, riding above fields of cows; they don't stop to think that we spend almost every minute on the vast sea, alone but for the occasional ship, although this time Mr Johnson did spy a whale. Otherwise it's the same, the same creaking and vibrations and weathers. The ripples that run through the frame of the ship, up its length and back again. Always the sea. Day and night, sea, sleep and food. Stay in as much as you can to keep out of the wind. Keep away from where you might inhale smoke, or soot worst of all. Fill the ship's pool. See the decks are cleaned on fine days if at all. Only when land nears, turn your mind to the port to come. The fields, cranes, the spires and towers, the mountains or the hills. Like here, the Harburg hills.

The *Hanjin* giant is turning faster, showing its bulb bow. Victoria lets the desk phone ring. Lets the papers on the table keep their secrets longer. She closes down the computer and returns to the window. Across the river a group of people on a passenger liner in dry dock has gathered at a rail to watch. Victoria wonders how many people still realise that very dock was where the keel was laid to the battleship *Bismarck*, seventy years before. She hadn't known until Paul mentioned it in his letter: the *Bismarck*, then the most heavily armed warship afloat, had left those docks for trials, then sailed back up the Elbe for final touches to be made. A flat floating arsenal, huge and mighty but not even half the tonnage of the *Hanjin Taipei*. Tugs would have turned the *Bismarck* right here, just like this. Five years to build and just nine days at war, before being battered and torpedoed to the bottom of the Atlantic.

So come on Merry, said Deborah looking straight at him as she shook the wrong end of the salt cellar, tell me exactly what you're doing. I'm still in advertising, he said watching the salt fly. Advertising what? All kinds of things, it hardly matters what; what I do is more about finding an approach, a slogan. So how would you advertise me, said Deborah. I— well you'd have to tell me about *yourself*. Me, hm, well, myself. I've some experience behind me, *too* much you could argue, too much to easily make one of those *profiles* people like, is that something that you do too? What are you saying? asked Merryweather tussling with the bones of his *Scholle*, what experience exactly? What do I mean? said Deborah indignantly, what do you mean, do you mean of men, are you trying to tie me up with men somehow? I didn't mean that, no, it was an open-ended question you might say. Merry, do you know how many men I've slept with? Twelve. Now that is enough exp*erience*. I knew a man once who said that was all he wanted to know, *how many*, can you imagine? Talk about quantity over quality. You know what I said to him? I said, "Is that 'how many' including you?", teasing him I suppose, because we hadn't, well, you know, hadn't. He couldn't answer my question so did I answer his? I didn't. I *pretended* to, just to see what would happen. I came out with some stupid number, like 'two'. He shut up, I shut up. He went his way, I went mine. Isn't that a line from a song, a jingle?

Stowaways, if there are any, often try the lifeboat at the stern. We find them, the port security doesn't. I'm not a fan of port precautions. Who likes gates and red tape? But Victoria will have to talk her way past the main booth if she is to visit. And someone will have to help her find her way across the maze of carriers and grabbers. Last week in Korea an engineer went down the gangway, looked left and was crushed by a van carrier coming from the right. Port time is only eight hours. Then back on the pendulum route as they call it, to Los Angeles. I told Mr Johnson she was coming. I didn't say she might not come at all. He cleared her visit insofar as he could. The crew won't like it, but they're changing anyway. Even if they see her, most of them aren't down for the return trip. There's such flux these days.

Troubled, Victoria puts her finger on what disturbs her. It's the fact she was looking out of the window at all. She never used to. She always got down to her work, listened, assimilated everything, argued, judged, decided. The organisation then worked as smoothly as it could. Now she was looking out of the window at a boat made in China, stacked with containers made in China, containers containing goods made in China.

One telephone stops, the other starts. Could be the same person. Waves from the turntabling manoeuvre slap at the quayside below. The second phone stops.

Three days with Paul had been delightful and that was all. *Did you love me for ever, just for those three days?* Paul wrote once. She thought that was clever until he revealed he was quoting from a song. Lucinda Williams, his sun in the sky. But had he come to grips with how she Victoria was? Her plans did not include lifelong love. There was no reason for them to match the way Paul would have liked. Once she realised that, she stopped replying to his notes; the notes he went on writing, like a bird singing for a mate not knowing all its kind are now extinct. She was trying to help him by not replying. She hears someone behind her. Her assistant has entered without knocking. The environment minister is on the line, Pirke says. The *minister*? Minister, says Pirke. Of course, says Victoria. Pirke hands her a mobile phone. She finds herself talking to him smoothly. Concentrating on his words. Agreeing about the draft they've both seen. Saying she stands by everything, yes, that's good of course. Yes. Carefully letting him close the conversation his way.

The ship is broadening across, approaching the point when its bow will be full on, the recesses of its anchors huge, a dozen containers spread across and its tall white bridge a flat wall, its windows squarely facing her.

Deborah went to the ladies' room. Merryweather stared at his own black coat on the coat stand. There's another container ship coming, the waiter said to him suddenly. I don't see one, said Merryweather turning to look down the Elbe. No, said the waiter, but it's coming; we're in direct contact with the *Dienststelle*, we have a deal with them. Really? said Merryweather. Yes really, said the waiter, those informations you can see on our monitor. We can tell our customers when a big ship is coming so they stay more time. Everyone is satisfied. Merryweather read the name *Cosco Guangzhou* on the monitor. How would it be, said the waiter, with a dessert?

We swing round fast, like a giant camera panning. We turn fastest at the stern as it's a long way back, on the outside of the turning circle. You have to turn yourself if you want to keep your eye on something. Swivel in your chair. Look there: Victoria could be working in one of those offices, could be one of those people looking.

I was shockingly in love with her. A shock like your very first of something wonderful. The first firework you've ever seen, bursting in a shower of glitter. Seeing your first kingfisher. Waking to a flower not there the day before. She glittered and flowered—and was gone. Too late I told her how I felt. Now she never replies. She asks for nothing. I could say here I am, come to you with thousands of tonnes of everything imaginable. Down there, Victoria—but so what?—I have artichoke hearts, a caravan, sandals, Egyptian fennel, marjoram and basil, axles, pumps, office chairs, ladies' wear, crockery, electrical goods, even the personal effects of a Mr and Mrs Nabarro of Otis, Oregon, weighing in at 7,297 pounds. A whole world, Mr Johnson likes to say, fits in one of these ships. Almost a whole world. But never enough for Victoria. Down there in a reefer, as they call the refrigerated boxes, are 20 tonnes of apples. It might as well be a million.

Are you happy living here? said Deborah, is it home? I suppose so, said Merryweather. And what are you doing here, said Deborah, you always were someone to do something different, how was your fish? Fish? I thought you'd never ask. Well you were wrong, said Deborah; how was it? Once I'd managed the bones it was good. An *odd*ball, we used to say about you. That's not very nice, said Merryweather. Nice? said Deborah, what is nice? Life is much too short—anyway mine is—to spend too much time being nice. I still don't know anything much about you and we've been here how long—my God, is that the time? I'm due to meet my sister at four. Plenty of time, said Merryweather. There's nothing wrong with being an oddball, Deborah went on. Victoria is an oddball too. She puts everything into her work, everything. She could have had so much, our mother said. Our mother said she could have travelled the world, had cars and houses galore, had sex to make her weak at the knees; and what does she do, she runs an international organisation with all its pains and heartaches, gets ill and goes back for more.

The bridge of the *Hanjin Taipei* is full on, directly facing, but the full length of the vessel away. A giant could hop to the bridge from container stack to container stack the way children play hopscotch. The vibrations of engines seem to be transmitted off the river bottom, up through the grey water to the office building. She catches a glint of light from one of the windows. Maybe Paul is just there.

She rolls her shoulders. The massed weight of the containers is audacious, bullish, God help us if the vessel should miss its turn. Victoria has an image of how the *Titanic* sank up on end, of how the *Bismarck* rolled onto its side and over. The foremast and the bridge, the mast with the radar scanner twirling, line up neatly with the bow. As if in a drawing. The windows at the bridge seem to glass over.

What's oddest of all, said Deborah, is that you and my sister end up living in the same place. And you don't even know each other. I met her once, said Merryweather. Look, said Deborah: Not to beat about the bush, I can feel what there is between us, believe me, and it's not—not enough, or do you want to beat about the bush because I don't. I like you, I really like you, but I don't fancy you, not because you may not have a hair left on your head, which you don't, but don't get a complex as it doesn't mean a thing, believe me. Accentuate the essentials, I say. So there you have it. As my dictionary says, wait, here: *erledigt*. Now can we move on to the dessert? Oh Merry, there's more of that rolling, oh do do that rolling act of yours one more time.

Mr Johnson wants me to check the cable. As if a pirate were shimmying up it. Back we go, back, back. People think pirates attack us on the high seas. But it's rare. You can't just *scale* a container ship. Even the pilots have trouble coming up the ladders and there we are trying to help them. I've heard people say I may get machine-gunned or thrown overboard. Mr Johnson says that's nonsense, at least on the pendulum route. He was held at gunpoint once, he says, and paid a ransom of sausages and cheese. In the West we're more likely to get cases like the paying passenger who went missing, whose sandals we found neatly together on the deck by the rail.

Both phones are ringing. Why answer this one rather than that? A face appears at the door and pretends to knock. Victoria shakes her head firmly. She switches the computer back on. The person at the door goes away. In the window the *Hanjin* carrier is pivoting perfectly. The second tug, the *Angelika*, is now closer. The tugs will have to stop pulling soon; change their manoeuvres to pull Paul away from her, back into the arm of the river and the bay of the terminal.

Back back we go. Mr Johnson says there is a message for me. *Good luck Paul, Victoria*. A message. I always wanted a message. Not this message, a different message. *Good luck Paul, Victoria* contains several messages. Unzipped, unwrapped, they can be laid out as: *Goodbye; we will not meet, ever; our lives have separate futures*. Unpacked further I see revealed *Best you remove me from your inner life*. What can I say? Or do? It's hardly worth taking a taxi into town; and back. And we have to sail out today. Tomorrow is Friday; every sailor knows it's bad luck to set sail on a Friday. Still, it was splendid coming those miles up the Elbe. No more creaking and plunging like at sea. The houses on the hill at Blankenese rose up like a fairy-tale town. Everyone felt like saluting, from the captain to the third engineer. Be reassured, said Mr Johnson pointing to the church towers; the towers mean continuity, that however much may have changed, much has remained. He has a comment for every situation. Container shipping has changed the world, he's fond of saying, especially if you're a gull. Because there's hardly a scrap to eat off a ship any more, it's all so tightly packed and sealed. We're docking. Slowly slowly. Clang, boom, twirling lights, orange everything. We're getting in new DVDs and a book or two. On the trip out Mr Johnson has promised us a talk on orang-utans, and an old-fashioned slide show of Angkor Vat. None of that relates to anything, but when you're on the sea it doesn't matter anyway. Out there it's the opposite of being on land: you're always taking stock, taking stock. It's that interspersed with the occasional emergency, an engineer who's been drinking too much, an argument over what film to show in the mess, a reefer that leaks. Without the orang-utans or Angkor Vat it would just be more of the same. Being on watch, checking, watching. Hearing the engines. The creaking and vibrations and weathers. It's good to look at the sky. Stay healthy, go to the pool. Keep out of the wind. See the decks are cleaned on fine days, if at all.

BLYTH

GENTLE ENGLISH WALBERSWICK, 1915. Quiet wealth and boat huts. Lupins, lavender. Sand, pebbles, dunes, crabs to catch on lengths of string. Fields of grazing sheep and cattle, beds of reeds, low marsh and calls of birds. Yawls on the beach and rowboats beside the River Blyth.

Straightening his long grey coat, removing his bowler hat, Albert Muldoon, MI5, comes, knocks and enters. Questions. In Walberswick, home among other homes to the paranoic populace of East Anglia, now at war. East Anglia, flat land, England's weakest point, where so many invasions have begun, so close to continental Europe. Come on, says Muldoon to his assistant as he brushes what looks like a flake of tobacco off his bowler, there's work to do. Work? MI5? For the painter Charles Rennie Mackintosh is a spy. Who else calls on your door and asks to draw a flower in your garden? Such a flimsy pretence. I am a spy, Charles Rennie foolishly jested at one door, a spy who paints. May I paint your fritillaria? It is so hard to find in the wild. Furthermore he is from Scotland. It is too early in the century for many to realise an adept spy should be indistinguishable from an ordinary person. Even the 1914 profile of a spy is vague. Can a spy be allowed to clean the local church, as Charles Rennie offered? Is a moustache a sign of a spy? The overflowing cravat he wears?

Albert Muldoon and his assistant, both in their bowlers, have come joking down the lane after a decent cup of morning tea in the tearoom by the green. And a lunchtime drink at the Bell Inn, where they listened to the rumours.

Mr Mackintosh takes long walks to nowhere beside the River Blyth. He leaves Millhouse at night, stops at the crabbing bridge in the dark. He trails along the beach carrying a lantern. Maybe signalling to a U-boat. He had been motored to Blythburgh and back for no fathomable reason. He drinks and sings songs nobody knows. And: he receives post from the Continent. Drink up, said Muldoon to his assistant, Baxter, as red-cheeked and bright-eyed as he is almost-sickly pale. That'll be the last real beer you'll sup in a while, they're going to water it to make it last longer. Asquith's doing, don't blame me. There will be a radio in that paintbox I bet, said Baxter before draining his tankard with his head back. No doubt, said Muldoon. You catch him out with your questions, a local voice advised, and we'll come and take him away for you. You'll see, he isn't like us. Not even like that Mr Steer he rents from, and he's queer enough. A painter too, he claims.

For Charles Rennie Mackintosh persecution is normal enough. They want to stop him being the artist he wants to be. His best work is trashed by critics. His architecture they call outmoded. He rarely shows his paintings. He ignores the critics but cannot so easily ignore the gentlemen from the MI5.

A spy? Unlike, say, the King, he has no connections with Germany—he says as much to Albert Muldoon, chief investigator up from London.

He lets them in. He waits for them to plant evidence against him, without knowing what this evidence could be.

Sit doon, Mr Muldoon. Why's yer colleague standin by the door like that?

So you don't run for it, Baxter said.

Whit wud "it" be? said Charles Rennie. This is ma hame and ah'll no be goin oot jist noo. Sit doon.

Come in Baxter, come in, said Muldoon. I'm listening.

Are ye noo.

What are you doing in Walberswick?

Paintin.

Why have you come here in particular?

Ah've a pal, Mr Steer, at Valley Farm. And ah wis familiar wi the area. Ah wis here a wee while in '97. You can say ah'm here on a recuperating holiday.

Here as opposed to say, Southwold. Or Inverness.

D'ye ken Inverness, Mr Muldoon?

I was in Scotland once. At a loch.

Loch Lomond?

Maybe.

Ah wurk here. Ah paint. Do ye want to see ma wurk?

Not particularly.

Ye dinnae want to?

I take it that is a painting by you on that wall.

Are the figures no very fine, ah widnae be at aw sorry if ah cud dae that. That's by Mr Steer. "Knucklebones", he calls it. It's bin loaned to me specially.

And that one? Is that a painting by you?

An auld wan, aye.

Where did you paint that?

In Glesga. There's even part of ma studio thur, see, back of the tulips. That's art, sure enough. Art is the flower.

I hear you were ousted from Glasgow. They say you got drunk and—became hard to manage.

There's truth to that, sure enough. Ah, this is Margaret, ma wife. Margaret, Mr Muldoon. He's frae the police.

MI5.

MI5. He thinks ah'm a spy.

Then ah'm a spy too.

Indeed, said Muldoon.

For aw ah ken, said Mrs Mackintosh, yer cud be a spy yersel.

Margaret.

Oh dear. Ah wis pure being humorous. Ah kin be a wee bit too sharp sometimes. But whit does a spy dae? Disnae a spy gather wee secrets? Hae connections? How's ma husband supposed to be a spy?

That is hardly a discussion I can enter into, Mrs Mackintosh.

Ma wife is a great support to me in ma wurk.

That I don't doubt.

She is an artist as weel.

Well. We will have to search your house, Mr Mackintosh. Mrs Mackintosh. I have the necessary papers. Even if I didn't have them I would still insist. We are at war.

Then ah will accompany ye. Ah've nothing to hide. Indeed ah dinnae have onythin to show.

Are ye takin ma husband somewhere?

No, Mrs Mackintosh. This is a preliminary enquiry.

So if ah wis goin away for a day or two ye widnae mind.

You are free to do what you want, Mrs Mackintosh. The state has no interest in law-abiding citizens. This is England, where it is the duty of a citizen to go about his or her business.

Ah'm glad to hear that of course. Ah'll be away then Charles, like we said.

You'll no be goin jist noo, Margaret?

Ah'll be hame at the weekend. Ah'll jist hae a private wee word wi' ye at the door.

This must be the studio, the purported studio. So Muldoon called it, following his assistant inside. Baxter opened a box full of tubes of paint. No radio. As Muldoon opened and closed drawers, Baxter looked for an age at a watercolour painting of a flower propped against the bookshelf.

Mr Muldoon, there's something not right about this picture, and I believe I've found out what it is.

What's that?

It's too big. 'Winter stock' it says. I'm thinking he's made those flowers bigger than they are.

If he made them at all.

Ah, that's a point. But if he didn't do them who did? That Mr Steer?

Everything's possible. People didn't fly for thousands of years. Now they do.

How do you mean, fly?

In aeroplanes.

Well yes, Mr Muldoon. But if they'd had aeroplanes before now, they would have flown.

Baxter.

What is it, Mr Muldoon?

Concentrate on our task. We'll move on. To the kitchen. Do you know what I've noted, so far? He has no money.

Can ah help ye there?

Thank you, Mr Mackintosh, we're best left to ourselves.

Like Mr Muldoon was saying, you won't fly away without an aeroplane.

I didn't say that, Baxter.

Ah'll be makin a fresh cup of tea.

Not yet, Mr Mackintosh, we're about to go to the kitchen ourselves.

Aw right. But I didnae get whit ye were sayin aboot an aeroplane.

Or a Zeppelin, Mr Mackintosh. I don't suppose you know what a Zeppelin is.

Och ah do surely.

They can reach these coasts of ours.

Can they now? Well ah widnae want that.

Two high-backed chairs in the kitchen. Tulips in a Chinese vase. Sketches of houses on Walberswick Green, of the crabbing bridge over the River Blyth. Fishermen's nets laid out. An old painting of the river with a windmill, under thick black clouds, heavily varnished, hanging on the wall opposite the cooker. Almost bare drawings of empty marshes, shoreline, cliffs, horizons, possibly the North Sea.

See this picture, Baxter.

It's the Bailey bridge across to Southwold.

Look what's written under it. *Rail bridge, intended for Chinese train.* What do you make of that?

I don't know. There's many a mile between here and China.

And many a spy, Baxter.

There's certainly enough drawing and painting around, Mr Muldoon. Did you hear what he said though, "loaned to me specially"? Mind you, he seems to know a bit about art, if that's what you call it.

Pictures.

I have to say I find it rather pleasing, all in all, Mr Muldoon. I could just see that jasimine on my wall at home.

Jasimine?

Jasimine, it says on it: jasimine.

Somebody's made a slip there, Baxter. We'll be sure that goes in our report, just in case it's significant. Now concentrate on what you see, Baxter. Whatever you come across may be vital.

I am, Mr Muldoon. I just wanted to say that as a spy, he'd be trained in all this, art and painting, is that right? Very cunning, if you ask me.

Spying is an act of great cunning, don't forget, Baxter. Did you look in that cupboard there by the sink?

No money in here, Mr Muldoon. Just a lot of sugar.

Sugar? Well I never.

I could do with some of that myself.

Exactly. Sugar's regulated by royal commission. As of a month now. Or else it comes from Germany. Where's he got the sugar from?

From the shop? Do you hear that commotion, Mr Muldoon?

Charles, Ah cannae go oot there.

Margaret. Whit's wi' ye, Margaret? Whit is it?

What's going on? Baxter?

Charles thir are men oot the end of the path. They are angry men, sayin dreadful things. Mr Muldoon, ye must go there and tell them to go away. They're nae guid folk. They hadnae ony business cursin and shootin that way.

Shouting?

Shootin. In their loud voices.

It's those soldiers from the Bell, Mr Muldoon.

I'll see to it, Mrs Mackintosh. You come with me, Baxter. Put your bowler on.

Ah dinnae understand, Charles, Ah dinnae understand whit's goin on.

It'll be fine Margaret. They've gone now, the sodgers. Ye kin go now. Ah'll be jist fine.

Ah dinnae want ye walkin oot at night, Charles. Ah dinnae come all the way fae Scotland to be a widow.

When do ah walk in the dark, Margaret? Two times in a week? Ye ken ah dinnae like walkin in the dark.

Well aw right. But ye be sure to take yer wee lantern. Hae yer wits aboot ye.

Ah will.

Ah'm so proud of yer flowers there, Charles. Wan day people will look at those flowers of yers, look at that veronica, and they'll be sayin Wawberswick, ah Wawberswick. Ye'll hae done these folk hearaboots a favour and them none the wiser.

Mebbe, Margaret. That's as like as mebbe.

Pub hours have been shortened as a war measure. The Germans have stopped us drinking, the irascible soldiers at the gate argued. And to top it all, that Mackintosh likes a drink himself, he was bound to have a store in there. Muldoon assured them this was not so. I've searched this house, he said. Now go back to your unit. Your homes. Would he arrest the spy? Not now. Not yet.

We're almost done.

I fancy a cup of tea now, Mr Muldoon.

All right, Baxter. Not that China tea, though.

Ah kin gie ye ordinary tea. Excuse me while ah pit the kettle on.

One question, Mr Mackintosh. You seem to be short on money.

Money? Ah widnae say that wis a business of yers.

Everyone is hoarding sovereigns, haven't you heard? The treasury is so worried about it they're issuing notes. But you don't seem to have a sovereign in the house.

It's a struggle. Ah'm haein to sell the odd paintin to pals of mine in Glesga. Ah pawned wan as weel. Ah wish ah hadnae hae to dae it.

So you have reason to take up offers from all quarters?

Ah dinnae want to be decoratin folk's hooses, if that's whit ye mean.

No. But you are well off for sugar.

Margaret runs the messages.

Runs the messages, yes. I see.

Ye can git almost everything you want from the wee shop on the green.

Mr Mackintosh, I'm sure you have a good reason for going on the beach with your lantern.

Ah do. Ye ken Whistler, Mr Whistler from America? Him that painted pictures in the dark? Mr Whistler the painter?

Another one.

Ye dinnae ken Whistler?

Would you explain the lantern?

Explain the lantern? Ah dinnae care for the dark. Ah like to see where ah'm goin. Wuid ye no use one yersel?

It's a fair cup of tea you make, Mr Mackintosh, isn't it Mr Muldoon. You wouldn't have some shortbread would you, I dare say your wife makes a good shortbread. With that sugar.

Ah dinnae hae no shortbread. That would be a grand luxury with aw that butter.

Indeed. I see it's gone very quiet out there.

It is. It's mostly a quiet wee toon. Ah widnae want it the ither way. It isnae busy nae mair. Did ye ken ships used to go all over from here, lang ago?

What ships?

Ships wi' wool, and grain. And salt, and herrin of course. Ships to Holland and France. To Belgium and Poland.

And Germany?

Oh definitely. Germany too.

Well, Baxter, this is an education.

Yes, Mr Muldoon.

But I believe we've come to the end of our visit.

Aye, ah kin feel it too. Whit'll ye be doin next?

I'll file my report.

Yes, we'll file the report.

Baxter, I'm talking.

You are.

Then we'll see. The war could be over by then.

No if we go eftir the Turks like we are. We should be concentrating closer to hame, not goin to the Dardenelles. It's jist madness.

Mr Mackintosh, a strategist in warfare. You kept this under a bush until now.

Ah read the papers. Ah ask ye, Mr Muldoon, whit are they aw thinkin? Constantinople isnae a hoose of cards. Ach, it dinnae allthegither matter. Either way it means a lot of war. Who kin ken whit oor foreign secretary Sir Edward really thinks? Did ye ken he wis here jist last year, oot burdwatchin they said. Lookin at wee burds hoppin aboot, with a war on. A war. War and misery—wifies and weans feart for their faithers and their faithers feart for a'thing else. A war is a war. It isnae goin to stop like a train in a station.

Quite, Mr Mackintosh. Get your hat, Baxter, and we'll be on our way.

Anyway, ah tell ye, ah'm too auld for aw that. Ah'm forty-six this year. Ah suppose ye think that isnae too auld for a spy.

Mr Muldoon and I can't really say. We've never met a spy. Well, not to our knowledge.

That's enough, Baxter. Don't pay my assistant any attention, Mr Mackintosh. This is new territory for him. We'll be going. Don't be reporting our visit to anyone. We may have to work under-cover in the future. Don't write our names down on any paper. Forget we were here. Tell Mrs Mackintosh the same.

When all the toon kens ye wis here? But aye ah will. It'll

no be wi' a happy heart, mind. So ye've seen everythin, said everythin?

I was indeed at Loch Lomond — at Aldochay.

Ach, ah had a feelin ye wis there, ah felt ye had somehow. Aldochay, di' ye say? Ah dinnae ken it. It must be awfa wee.

My wife is from there. Goodbye. Lock your door at night, Mr Mackintosh.

Ah will that. Ah always do. This is England, so ye tell me. It's a funny message which ah cannae help but notice. But if this is the way an artist is gone aboot in this country, ah'll be pittin ma lock on by day as weel.

Yes yes, Mr Mackintosh. I'll be saying goodbye for the time being. I advise you to stay calm.

When a group of soldiers entered the house in Walberswick rented by Charles Rennie Mackintosh he is said to have raved at them in such a fury that the soldiers, astonishing as it sounds, mistook his Glaswegian for German, arrested him on the spot and threw him into jail. Only after his wife's resolute efforts in proving him not to be a German spy was he released a week later. Nonetheless the Mackintoshes were directed to leave the East Anglian counties; in 1915 he and Margaret moved to Chelsea in London.

AIRE

ONCE I HAD the idea for a book involving rivers they duly appeared everywhere. For most of the roughly two years I spent writing these stories and pulling them together I was in either Hamburg or Suffolk. From my desk at work in Germany I saw the Elbe, restless with ferries and container traffic; in Suffolk the Deben was in view, its bends graced by oystercatchers, swans, shelducks and the occasional red ochre sail. For brief stays I was in Amsterdam, Paris, London: to visit a city is to be aware of its river.

The television series *Coast* used to delight in regularly pointing out that 'in the UK you are never more than 72 miles from the sea' (although people in Warwick maintain they would need to go a few miles more). The distance to the nearest river—with over three hundred of note in the UK alone—will be much less. And, driving or walking, we seek them out. According to a recent survey, one in three walks are valued because they include water.

I am grateful to the friend of mine who pointed out that the way rivers cut through land presents a curious paradox: met side-on they can be a barrier; taken lengthways they offer a conduit. In part because of this, we know them in so many guises: as water to cross, travel along or admire. Smaller rivers are often places to enjoy, while the great waterways remain a highway for commerce. They are carriers of waste and homes to animals, plants and disease. Again, however much they change their looks or shape, we see them as links with the past. Even as material for jokes like that made by Mark Twain: *Denial ain't just a river in Egypt.*

Meanwhile, oblivious to human exploits, the rivers themselves continue.

A great many rivers occurred to me for the stories brought together in *As Rivers Flow*. One, the Mersey, I knew as a young child. We clanked thrillingly across it on the old Runcorn transporter, fearing the family Prefect, later a Vauxhall, might somehow roll off, or the cables of the transporter snap and the platform tumble into the chilly brown ripples of shallows and mud down below. We looked at the bleak tarpaulins of water from the promenade at Otterspool. Or took the ferry Gerry Marsden later famously sang about. To a child the broad lanes, curves and lights of the Mersey Tunnel are unforgettable, although that heavenly lighting was recently overhauled and removed. But I had no story to go with the Mersey, which for a year remained mere fragmented pictures and ideas.

Another story I came close to setting down involved the Alde in Suffolk. Two men in a Canadian canoe took to its wide reaches under a stormy sky. A canoe is a private space, like that of a car, in which movements are confined and little can be said face to face; an opportunity for disclosing secrets and intimacies. The two men found themselves telling each other of momentous decisions in their personal lives. But while knowing a subject is normally a help in telling a story, here the problem was the opposite. I knew the real-life version too well. It dampened the place where the necessary creative spark might have been struck, and no story caught alight. Sometimes the biggest ideas become salvaged only as the tiniest minutiae: this pair did at least make the briefest of cameo appearances in *Stour*.

There was the little mountain river wending through the village of Croesor in North Wales—a place of extraordinary goings-on, known to poets, writers, painters, long ago the

Romans and more recently even the BBC; a handful of houses and cottages until recently dominated by three like-wise extraordinary women. I knew of the deserted slate-mining village up the valley; of a woman in a white cottage with a black horse, a bull rolling down the mountainside. But still no story came.

Turning to the Thames and its dozens of tributaries, there was the Cherwell in Oxford, English and sun-dappled, a precious bubble of a place for students immersed in the thrills and bewilderments of their so-young relationships; the Fleet, one of London's 'shadow rivers', buried under-ground but apparently still capable of flooding the odd basement along its course. Again no story came. In a fiction not for publication I depicted a hippy family enamoured by the Windrush in the Cotswolds, its oxbow bends and flood meadows. Of the tributaries entering the Thames only the Kennet appears here.

Across the Atlantic, I pictured the roaring Fraser river in British Columbia; the toughest men and women, a hermit in a damp rainy forest. The brown Napo in the full-verdant Ecuadorian Amazon, deliriously lush to the point of beck-oning people towards feverish action, or even death (*Yo me voy a matar*, a song about the Amazon goes). Finally I imag-ined another very different canoe trip, with three women paddling, water dripping in sparkles down their arms, amongst the swank villas on the glassy canals of the Alster in Hamburg. Nonetheless, the tale with the Windrush apart, these were all, for whatever reasons, stories that did not get written.

The story I would most dearly like to have told, or rather re-told, was set down by John Buchan in the early 1920s. 'The Flight to Varennes' appeared with other Buchan tales in *A Book of Escapes and Hurried Journeys*. The river was the

Aire, not the Yorkshire Aire passing through Skipton and Leeds but a hundred mile long river in France, to the east of Paris and halfway to what now is Belgium. It joins the Aisne, then the Oise, and eventually the Seine. A bridge over the Aire was as far as the imperilled Marie Antoinette and Louis XVI one night managed to flee from Paris.

Despite journeying in a great yellow *berline* coach, the one means of transport the king was accustomed to, historians claim he and the queen nonetheless cleared two hundred miles before being seriously challenged. Buchan mesmerisingly tells the tale of their flight, which he said he researched from fifteen different sources.

The adrenaline of the royals flows from the start. First a smaller carriage to take them out of Paris—known then as a 'glass coach'—waits on a quiet street. On her way to it Marie Antoinette fears she has been spotted in the shadows. Flustered, she loses her way and becomes delayed in the dark alleys around the Tuileries. A fateful half hour lost, she finally reaches the glass coach; now the royal party will miss a crucial rendezvous with loyal troops at Somme-Vesle.

As they change to the great *berline* with its eleven horses, yellow livery and white velvet upholstery; as it stops in a forest for them to debate what to do next, or takes to a hazardous hillside road, Buchan tells us in detail of how the pressure mounts—of the route, the allegiances of the towns they pass, the coach rumbling and rolling, crashing through trees, fording water, stopping to have the green blinds pulled down, drawing up by an inn. Hounds are heard baying. Eventually, encountering growing opposition from the common people, the king and queen have to turn back at the Aire and retreat abjectly to the fates awaiting them in the capital.

Aire: that is the story most missing from *As Rivers Flow*, but it cannot be told more finely than it was by John Buchan the best part of a century ago.

SEINE

WINTER HAS REACHED Paris. On its northern curve, the grim cupola of the Panthéon is gathering a film of snow. Skin, were it to touch the icy dome, would stick to its metal and stone.

When the philosopher (teacher of Pascal, Descartes) leaves the apartment below the cupola wearing two scarves, he will carry only a few books with him, into the snow and the night.

The books include Rayuela, the Paris novel by Julio Cortázar, Borges' Ficciones, Antonio Tabucchi's Petits Malentendus Sans Importance (Little Misunderstandings of No Importance) and a book on Manet by Georges Bataille.

The lift continues past the floor with the blocked-up exit. The cage jolts to a halt. He feels his heart. In place of a sturdy beat he feels a sagging sack, slung loosely under his ribs. Yet when the door to the street closes behind him he will step out with a desperate yearning.

The snow is light and wet. Thin flakes melt on his cheeks.

A lone man, talking, passes by.

The philosopher tugs one scarf tighter.

Stopping under a soft street light, he thinks of Bulle Ogier in the film La Salamandre, as she sits on the side of a bed and turns to the tall man:

I want

I want to sleep

I want to sleep in your bed

I want to sleep in your bed with you

He longs to hear words like these, strange words until now only encountered in a story told in snow, in Switzerland. He's seen many films, felt the twists of millions of conversations, billions of words.

I want to

Who would ever speak such words to him now?

He hears groans. He imagines hands stepped on in the dark. The terrible life sleeping out in the rue Cujas.

Those sudden downfalls.

Ceausescu. Napoleon. Zhivago.

Struggling life. In the deltas of Bangladesh. In Palestine.

Even China. The Great Wall of China — the subject of a newspaper clipping he has with his books — is falling down.

Closing his eyes, he wishes the Panthéon would turn into a glass hothouse smelling of woodsap and ferns. When he opens his eyes it is still massive and ugly. A building of the French empire, surely soon to disappear.

Stamping his feet in the cold, looking to the very top of the dome, the philosopher feels his neck hurt. He also feels a joy, for despite leaving Marianne, with nowhere to go, he delights in being a tiny creature. Were it not for the clouds, galaxies could register on his retina. A speck of nothing; yet able to contemplate vast things, clusters of stars, empires, centuries of human history.

After years of living with Marianne, he remembers just a handful of things that she said.

I want to sleep

I want to sleep in your bed

I want to sleep in your bed with you

Not with Marianne.

Her tales jarred. She told him she dreamed of a horse, an owl and the sex of a woman. The day after this dream one of her students gave her a Celtic coin displaying these very things. This disturbed him (teacher of Pascal, Descartes). But not the coincidence, nor the coin (she lied: who had a Celtic coin?). What disturbed him was: why tell him she dreamed of the sex of a woman?

Sex had become something they both only dreamt of. He decided to leave.

He had other reasons to leave. Because they had not had a vibrant conversation for years. Because they sat at the same table but without appetite. They talked, but without enthusiasm. Otherwise they kept out of each other's way. Their interests were exclusive. They agreed only on matters of no consequence. Their lives were Ficciones. They had Little Misunderstandings of No Importance.

More months passed before he gathered a few books and put on two scarves and his long black coat and went down in the lift and out in the cold.

To stamp his feet, to send warm blood to his toes. The cold is at its most bitter in the rue Cujas. It moves off the Seine up the rue St Jacques.

One third of the Great Wall of China is now flush with the ground. The stones have been used by local people for shelter, pigsties and coal mines. Another third is collapsing. Once visible from space, even a Chinese astronaut has confessed it can no longer be seen.

Can the Panthéon be seen from space?

Emperor Ming built the wall as a defence. But what is it for now? What is the Panthéon for now?

He looks past the great pillars, to the great doors. Why a mausoleum in the centre of a city? This city has lost its way.

The energy is seeping from it. Even the city Cortázar described, a place of chance encounters and streets with tantalising names such as *rue de Nevers, rue de la Clef*, has gone. There has been confusion and much fumbling: the baton of energy has been dropped. It was carried by Manet as he painted enigmas, flowers, gazes, while enjoying the salons. Haussmann created his avenues, then Eiffel his tower. Lautrec, Curie, Piaf, De Gaulle. 1968. La Défense. La Musée d'Orsay. It was close to Orsay that the baton was dropped into the Seine, the black Seine, with barely a splash, the weakest plop. Today Haussmann's avenues and star-shaped intersections, physical survivors, go unfrequented by pedestrians, have disappeared from people's minds.

The coffee in Paris has watered over time. The wine has been mixed. The mayonnaise now comes crinkly out of tubes.

China: crumbling. Hiroshima: melted. Pompeii: dust. The Renaissance—a hobby of the philosopher—at least combined optimism with grandeur. But the Renaissance crushed Italy under its weight. Under the buildings, the paintings of popes and angels. No one would emulate those paintings for centuries, why even try?

Old buildings, the Panthéon, his ragged heart. Imagine a baton of iron deep in the sludge of the Seine.

Where to next?

At the corner with the rue St Jacques he turns up his collar to a squall.

Through the sleet he spies a section of railings, majestic, like a ship at the end of a street: the Luxembourg Gardens.

His newspaper clippings include an old article about them. It is twenty years since anyone succeeded in staying overnight there. Henri Roquin, a civil servant who lost his entire family when a dock wall collapsed in Marseilles, spent the night in a tree, until a gardener discovered him.

The philosopher has with him dozens of newspaper cuttings, collected over the years.

He watches his own breaths.

He discounts going to the Luxembourg and all gardens. Above all he discounts returning to Marianne. Leaving him with hotels, of which there are many nearby.

He takes a last look at the Panthéon in its shroud of weather and spotlights by night, snow flurrying around the cupola. He is convinced there will be black ice on the walls of its catacombs. Encasing Voltaire, Zola, Dumas, more thickly still in their vaults. So many frozen bones. Decaying all the more slowly in the cold, to crumble all the more rapidly once it stops. And what for, what is the sense to the Panthéon now? Only one purpose occurs to him. If he jumped from the upper gallery he would bounce on the cupola and be caught inside the balustrade of the lower gallery. From there he could clamber to the arch with its gold AUX GRANDS HOMMES LA PATRIE RECONNAISSANTE. Then, one final look: Notre Dame, Sacré Coeur, the flashing beacon of la tour Eiffel, dark lighthouse in the midst of no sea and no ships. He would slide past the gutter through space to hit the steps below.

He turns his back and walks quickly downhill, however, studying the fronts of the hotels. Men in beards are in the foyers. He has no beard. He waits outside one hotel to see a man with no beard. Finally he sees a black man without a beard wearing an enormous violet ring.

Staring through the window, he touches the pane. A receptionist meets his stare and picks up the phone.

He decides to walk all the way to the Pont des Arts, and is soon at the bottom of the rue Soufflot, soon crossing the boulevard St Germain, soon—but as he passes the end of rue de la Harpe and takes in its cheap coloured lights, cheap restaurant fronts, his sack of a heart goes taut. In the very rue de la Harpe, as a young man, in a hotel room with thin walls, he loved a young woman he greatly desired.

But already he walks on. He is soon striding alongside the Seine, feeling the vapour from its water entering his lungs. His breaths make fogs.

He jumps
In his mind he jumps
In his mind he throws in his books and jumps
In his mind he throws in his books
He doesn't jump
Looks for his books, which he's lost. The Seine is black. He holds his breath to look at the space where the water has to be.

After centuries of art, he told Marianne, only Goya and Manet could paint black. She told him to keep his thoughts to himself. Paint black, so what, Jean-Luc, she said hating him. And don't come near me tonight.

He looks at the black, where the black would be. He breathes fog in, fog out. He studies the fogs forming and dispersing, fogs with short lives. He looks out along the Seine as it forks at the Ile de la Cité. He desires, desires what?

His mind turns to another conversation with Marianne; about a situation in a book. A man is at a bedroom window looking at a storm, and a woman in the bed calls to him. He showed Marianne the passage. Tapping the page he said to her, desperate: Will you do what the character in this book does (*character*? she said scornfully, *book*?)? Look: He is at the window, looking rapturously at a storm approaching. Rain has begun entering the room, but he is unconcerned. The woman wants him to leave the storm and be with her. *Viens au lit*, she says.

Marianne said, What has this to do with me? The storm, he said persisting with his explanation to its end, created a sexual charge (with *you*? *sexual charge*?). So? The man shut the window. Nonetheless, the book says, the man would never forget the storm. He cannot forget it because her love-making was so magnificent.

I want to sleep

I want to sleep in your bed with you

Bulle Ogier said this sat on the Swiss man's bed. It was a similar situation to the one in the book.

Would her love-making have been magnificent? There is surely a place for magnificence.

But not in winter in the night on the Pont des Arts.

The instructor (Tao) stayed in the lotus position and put a cushion beneath herself.

I will live better without him, she said to herself. He meant trouble and pain. Worse, boredom. If he throws himself in the river tonight I will be chagrined for a day, then I will get used to the fact, then I will be glad of the fact, then I will forget the fact. What fact? What husband?

She put her palms together. She should seek to clear her mind.

But he won't. I will be doing all the throwing. I will throw away his books. His desk. His pictures. The vases he liked. The rugs he walked on. His car is too big to throw away. I will trade it for a nice second hand Citroen.

With her palms still together she turned her hands until one was beneath the other, like plates of the earth. She slid the bottom hand away from the top hand.

I will throw them away whatever he does. That print of the angels with the fish over the sofa. Why ever is that angel carrying a fish in that strange cradle of string?

Jean-Luc said the angel is anxious not to lose the fish. Don't forget the fish.

Her final remark to him was almost: don't forget the fish. She was ready to yank the picture off the wall and thrust it into his hands. But at the very last moment, as he stood wrapping a scarf around his neck, checking his pockets, she said nothing.

The door shut quickly and without ceremony, in the tap of a fingernail. She heard the lift arrive. It shut dully, like a clasp. It clanked going down.

He was gone, at last gone.

Studiously, seeking the discipline she was failing to find, and so the air she breathed would reach the small of her back, the instructor inhaled. With her left hand tucked close to her chest, she gradually moved her right arm far to her right, until it was stretching to the furthest corner of the world. To New Zealand, across all the places and people in between. Further. She had only reached rice fields in Cambodia. She was gathering energy. She strove to go as far as she could go.

His electric sander. Those tweezers he used to pull the hair out of his ears.

The philosopher turns away from the chill of the river. He will walk to Châtelet, take the RER to Paris Nord. Go north. To the coast, no. To his sister's near Calais, no. To a friend's house, maybe. He walks quickly, but inattentively. Somehow he has crossed to the wrong side of the river and is somehow on the rue St André des Arts, somehow walking behind an American (he assumes) girl on the rue St André des Arts. Sprouting from the backside of her blue jeans, hamburgered backside, is a shining white miniature copy of The Little Prince. He imagines walking past her to glimpse her face. He imagines returning to the Pont des Arts. Walking on the Great Wall of China.

There is no Great Wall of America. There are Great Lakes. The Great Divide.

America may die in its sleep.

The instructor exhaled slowly as her hand returned from over Japan, bringing energy to her heart, which is where it was needed. Yet as she moved over the vastnesses she had trouble crossing the Himalayas, after suddenly remembering the sight of Mallory's body on Everest from a film she had seen on television, his bare back like marble. She ended her exercises and went to the window of her bedroom, where she looked out at the great dome of the Panthéon.

Would Jean-Luc return?

How many times would she look at the Panthéon railings and think she was seeing him walking there? Dozens, hundreds, none? When she went out, would she start avoiding certain streets, corners, cafés, because Jean-Luc might be there?

If she crossed paths with someone who looked like him, would she look away?

She went to the print with the angels in the living room and turned it to the wall. If Jean-Luc came back (should she change the locks?): she imagined him standing in the middle of the room, still in his black coat, looking out of place. Where is the fish, Jean-Luc could say. She: What fish?

The angels and fish were now a brown board with a label saying Filippino Lippi and a big price in French francs, hanging from a dark wire which had rubbed its rust on her fingers. Would he try to turn the picture back around?

She earmarked it as an object to turn on the next time she felt rage.

She watered the plants. The watering took her back to the bedroom window and the Panthéon lit up in the night. The pillars around the dome were creased elephant trunks. The lines of the outermost pillars bowed outwards against the night sky. They would soon collapse under the weight of the great dome, the rings of stone.

The philosopher makes decisions. He will spend the night in a hotel on the right bank of the Seine, so as not to risk meeting Marianne, with whom, his sack of a heart tells him, all desire had come to an end.

The philosopher's eye could embrace the universe; now his mind, likewise tiny, in a short moment contemplates the span of his remaining years.

He would stay in the hotel while he looked for a flat to rent. He would rent this while he looked for an apartment to buy. He would live there until he was too old to climb the stairs. He would sell the apartment and buy a ground floor apartment. He would sell that and rent a ground floor room. He would stay there until he was too stupid to cook a saucepan of mushrooms. By that time he would know what to do when, on a dark night painted by Manet, he would return with a book to the Pont des Arts.

He takes the rue Serpente, the boulevard St Michel. Soon he is crossing the end of rue de la Harpe, where he loved the young woman. She wanted to sleep in his bed. He remembers this rarely, but always the memory moves him.

DEBEN

THE VIRGIN TRAIN bent against a corner, a two-carriage train on a tight bend. The air outside the window was as clear as a song by Buddy Holly. Pairing him with the air was easy; he must have been in it, sharing particles: melding since Ipswich. I didn't fight that, I took it as it came. The next moments saw the arrival of a Virgin Anglia railways platform alongside. Its waiting-room painted by sunlight, the station had the intimacy of a quiet Holly song. I relaxed seeing a station shouldering a two-minute tune. Passengers got in and out; a real whistle got blown; the platform with its name-boards slid westwards to a descending guitar run. Still the air insisted on accompanying, putting sparkle on greenhouse glass and tractors bunched in a farmyard; on peaceful cattle which in the matter of trains had probably only ever seen slow-moving Virgins. Buddy the air fell on all these, even dipped into a long-stretching Anglia railways cutting. He was impregnating the scenery: taking over: no he wasn't. The cutting rose up, swallowed itself in its own darkness. The last of his air got shed in a tunnel. The scene changed. The train rode above an estuary of mud. A river lounged in ooze. Its course was a wet brown kite-tail. A plain opened its face under Virgin Anglia's sky.

Things had changed fast, a natural barrier had been tunnelled under. I did more old-fashioned looking around, through the window. This side of the hill felt almost raunchy, almost. The feeling added by the sky was gold streaks and white streaks, an expensive look, stormy, well-lit from somewhere. Diagonals ruled. Under the streaks came the flopped kite-tail and beside it blue woodland in bar shapes, sliced up by firebreaks. Somewhere there my brother Ray lived. It was my first blue forest ever, so I sat up straight while I thought on this. Five or six bars of untellable acreage were trimmed as tidily as Buddy was tidy, Buddy again. Buddy was so tidy it killed him. Yearning to clear his backlog of washing, get his trousers pressed, get the fluff from Iowa brushed off his stage suit before it was seen again in Minnesota, he chartered that plane and flew into the snowy night and it killed him. He was moving, risking, striving to gain cleaning-time. *Well all right*, he sang, *we will live and love with all our might.*

Buddy Holly and I were travelling by Anglia railways to my brother Ray.

I showed my back to the expensive looking sky and got up to examine the polythened map on the cream carriage wall. There I stood, keeping a glancing eye on my seat, on the motions of the rural track and the hills. The passengers, teenagers who had turned their seats into sofas, ignored me. It made a good place to think. I think too much, I've been told. If I ever come across a book called How To Think Less I should buy it without giving it a thought. I allowed the map of Suffolk to fill my mind.

This was pre-Virgin and crawling with green and grey details. I expected bacteria to start moving in its clay pits and heathland, tiny flies to take off and land at the US air bases. Now Buddy Holly was a *star*. Think on that word, star. A fine word, a success story of a word if you feel a parental-strength responsibility towards how words behave, if, like me, you get upset if they're sullen or just lazing about. Star: shining through the dark; bright, accompanying. Many people do not know the luminous sound of Buddy Holly and they walk with their heads down, in and out of shops and home to their televisions. They have no need of stars. I would not say these people include my brother Ray, who had the new music when he was a teenager, when the age of ten was a grey blimp on my distant horizon. Now I was travelling to visit him and his wife Veronica; their children, Ned and Caroline.

The map in the carriage had no index of places. I looked for Akenfield, the Suffolk village, the book, the *famous portrait of an English village* which some say was a real village but not really called Akenfield. So I was looking not for Akenfield, but for the real place under the name. That's me sometimes: working at decoding Akenfield backwards, on an OK summer's day, hurting no one. Having the real name begin with *Aken* or end in *field* would be too simple. Unless doublethink was at work. There were a lot of hams on the map. Metting-ham, Debenham, Rendlesham. It might end in *ham*. Or *burgh*, though burgh sounded too crowded for an out-of-the-way village. I ascribed thick certainty to the idea it would keep the three syllables of A-ken-field. The writer had to be able to transpose the real name and the false in his head as he wrote. I vowed to crack this puzzle and turned back to my seat.

I never did crack it, but sitting down I was still repeating bits of place names out loud to the air, crazily, going unheard through the phones and music of the teenagers with their feet on the seats: Coddenham, Redisham, Akenfield. What could Buddy make of this? His mind was far away. He expressed a desire to smoke. Back in 1999 smoking was still allowed in some Virgin carriages, but not on this train. Buddy was nervous. He knew Texas and a good portion of the mid-West, New York, London, Washington DC. Places that swirled and vibrated and smoked and shed skins every minute. But not much small-town England had coincided with his experience to this date. He had been in Cardiff, Sheffield, Doncaster—but venturing here wasn't easy for him. He had never been this far east, had heard it was well known for sand and mud. He was not a mud person; mud had no message for him; he was for white marble and clean sparkling water. So his normally outgoing self clung to his roots. He preoccupied himself with the Powerglide transmission of his Chevy Impala and thoughts of absent guitars. I felt for him, late and great that he was. Surrounded by a carriageful of sweatshirts and short jackets, unable to decide if he should keep his dark blazer buttoned or unbuttoned, he had to stay true to Ike, his mom and dad. He wanted to smoke, and smoking induced him to go and stand on the metal plates between the carriages.

That meant more moments alone in East Anglia. Leave me alone and I have these thoughts, melancholy nothings. I stared out of the window and tried to think less. I stared at the wind sucking away blue snatches of smoke at the end of the corridor. I followed everything this cigarette smoke had to offer, from the regular snatches to the wisps that stood almost still and grey and purple, the set of clipped rings that went up vertically. My travelling companion, smiling with bright intelligence, came back to our seats smacking his face with eau-de-cologne. I took another admiring look at the streaks in the sky, the blue bars of forest.

Wrinkling his nose to help push back his thick-rimmed glasses, Buddy swung down from the rack a sack of laundry which he hoped to deal with during the visit. He was just starting to show me the leatherwork he'd done as presents for Ned and Caroline when the train slowed for our station.

On the one side, the platform. On the other, halyards on their aluminium boat masts made their tinkling sounds — the River Deben. Buddy brightened. Sometimes he's a loner, sometimes he likes people. He buttoned and unbuttoned the blazer a last time and sprang down to the platform. Ray greeted us. A thin Veronica with hair shorn gave me the kiss on both cheeks. Ray had the same black beard but the chunky Celtic look had got thinner. The lost family fat had all found its way to Ned who, Ray pointed out, seemed to be stood watching for geese flying over with his hands in his pockets.

He's fifteen, said Ray as Ned looked away. Fifteen, Irwin.

Fifteen, I said conspiratorially. Ned?

Buddy, said Ray, this is a surprise.

Ray bid Caroline say hello. She skipped forward and back in a way that made Buddy call her a firecracker.

Here, Ray said, let me take that bag off you. Well thank you sir, but it's real easy to carry across a parking lot, especially a lot this size — it's not a lot, you could say, it's a little. I *knew* you would come with *some*body, said Veronica. Oh *yes*, said Caroline holding my hand and skipping still.

Buddy and Ray and I walked through the town. A bending street climbed the hill. Old houses bulged and leaned. There were shop windows in timber-frame fronts. Pink, sky blue walls. Enamel plaques for office premises. Next to London the town of Ray, Veronica and their children had an uncluttered feel, of spaces no one was thinking of filling.

It's kinda stately round here, said Buddy perusing a noticeboard of church service times. No dynamite looking for a fuse. I don't suppose it ever goes hog-wild. You guys ever make it to Lubbock, you can cruise around the Hi-D-Ho. I got some neat outfits you can try out for an evening.

A red jacket you all would go down a skunk in.

I'm sure it would be a ball, I said moving to meet Buddy's talk.

Yeah, a ball. Then we could compare notes.

Here's much quieter, said Ray. As you say, stately. We can get very stately in the country in England. Though things improved with Diana.

Diana?

We're continually fighting against getting encrusted.

Encrusted? Well hell.

We passed a shop window crammed with second-hand items.

Hey can I get a pipe in there? said Buddy. Let me go in and go see. Phil Everly has this crazy pipe, the kind you see old men in leather shorts smoking in Bavaria or Switzerland. Meerschaum, is that what they call it? I'm gonna see what I can come up with, I'll find you guys—he said as he buttoned his blazer and stepped towards the shop with an enormous grin—I guess no one ain't ever gonna get themselves lost round these parts.

We strolled on slowly.

The thing is, said Ray eventually, Veronica and I aren't getting on any more. Don't sleep together. Sometimes we don't even eat together. I've decided to leave.

This is very sudden, Ray.

It's not sudden. Just tedious. Painful. It's been on the cards a long time. I could have warned you . . . you didn't expect to walk into a family drama.

He took a very deep breath and stared up the street.

Here comes Buddy already.

Look at that craftsmanship, isn't that cool. He says it's gonna smoke soft and cool, soft and cool. Look at the shape and the bowl. I saw it and I wanted it. I can't wait for anything—you ask my friends Jerry or Norman or Bob. Ask my brothers. Ask Echo McGuire.

What about Peggy Sue? asked Ray. Is she real?

Peggy Sue Gerron? Sure she's real. But she never was my girl.

He stopped to take off his glasses. Echo was my girl, he said wiping his eyes. It didn't work though, he said blowing on the lenses. It was kinda sad. Holy cow, look at that cherrywood there. I got a real shell case and all. I can't wait to try it. I got everything right here. This pipe was made for this tobacco.

Let's get a drink at the pub.

Yeah, let's go in and let me smoke the place out. You got a good fire department in these parts?

After Buddy had moved from a Coke to Guinness to grappa ('don't anyone set a match to this hooch'), we tried to walk off our drinks. We came to a tall bridge over the railway and looked down on Virgin trains passing. The line bent around without a sleeper out of place, confidently, begging to find its way into a children's book. Down through the trees, I pointed out, is the River Deben.

That is *purty*, he said breathing deeply. Sure is purty. A boat out sailing and all, look at that cute little red sail. Rivers and I go together better than icing to a donut. Are we going down there, because we better do it quick. Stare at a bunch of water, my mom says, and when you look up the doggone world has moved all around. You folks got a boat?

Actually no, said Ray.

What do you guys do for fun?

Ray's having a hard time, I said.

Buddy looked thoughtfully at the tracks and tapped his pipe cautiously on the parapet. Looking just as thoughtfully in the river's direction, he said he appreciated our walk. Darn it, he said. He appreciated the view and even what looked like mud down there. He appreciated looking down on the cutting and the engineering of the curve going nicely into the distance; but he wanted to get on the phone. I gotta get the contracts sorted out. I gotta see to my clothes. Veronica said she'd see to them, and it's real good of her, but I don't know if she's gonna get far enough fast enough. And I gotta call my lawyer, get those contracts changed. Hurry and get on the train. Or a plane. Oh boy, I'm running right out of time. Can I get a plane round here?— someone told me I could. I gotta be back with the guys.

Buddy, I said. There's time. Your lawyers will still be at their breakfasts.

Well hell. I guess so.

We can walk along the river and stop at my office, said Ray consulting his wristwatch. The Deben is as fine as anything you have in Texas, I'm sure. You can call your lawyer from there.

Sounds good, said Buddy. Like my mom says, we sure would be in a mess without our telephones.

Ray sat on the sofa, staring.

Mu-um, da-ad, who is going to help me with my homework? said Ned stomping through the hall.

Buddy grabbed Caroline's arm and twirled her round. Let's you and me jive, he said to a squeal of delight.

I went to the kitchen to make tea on the corn-coloured Aga stove.

Now I realise this is not an easy question right now, I heard Buddy saying in the living room, but is my laundry—?

The laundry! said Veronica horrified, I forgot all about it.

I'll put it in the machine right now.

No no it's OK, I'll take it with me. I have to hurry on anyway. Now a man in the shop said I can charter a plane from, where is it, Mildenhall? I got an address here. I should try this number.

The American air base? That's quite a way from here.

So I'll see if I can't fix it up, just take these things with me, it'll save me the best part of a day.

What's the hurry? said Ned. Are you on drugs? Coke?

Yessir, I'll take a Coke any day.

Ecstasy?

Ned! said Ray stopping on his way to the kitchen—You have just said goodbye to your pocket money. I don't believe you said that. It's all that TV. Sex and drugs and rock'n'roll.

Have you ever had drugs? Ned repeated to Buddy with eyes shooting flame at his father.

Ned! That's enough.

Had drugs? No sir, I believe I have not.

But you're in a great hurry.

We US boys just pitch on in, that's all. Gotta get going, who knows when it might just end. You're buzzing around like a fly from some flowers to an ol' piece of meat and somebody whomps you. So you gotta get going.

I'm so glad you've been here, said Veronica. Such a gentleman. A model to our children.

Well thank you, that's good to hear. Sure is. Can I use your telephone?

Ray handed me a shiny chrome tea caddy. Waiting for the kettle I admired the great enamel-topped cupboard, salvaged by Ray from a sale of fittings from the HMS Ganges. The kitchen had something to admire on every side. Ray took out a tray.

It won't be easy leaving all this, I said stroking a toecap at the floor tiles.

No, said Ray supporting himself with his hands on the table, his face close against a vase of marguerites.

I worked so hard to put the whole place together, Irwin. I like it here. So my son is an upstart. But fifteen year olds are upstarts. My wife. My wife doesn't hate me. She's just indifferent. I don't care if she hears me.

Da-ad, said Ned appearing with a worn textbook which he held with the pages open, down by his side. Mum won't help me with my homework.

What? said Ray in dazed response.

It's about statistics.

Statistics? We've been through that already. Probabilities and throws of the dice.

No, it's nothing like that with the dice. We have to say what these figures mean.

I looked at the book. *Give your interpretation of these figures by answering the following questions.*

For instance, said Ned, here are the casualties in the North American Civil War.

Oh God, said Ray.

Da-ad.

I'll try and help, I said. Your dad'll finish making the tea.

Thanks Irwin, said Ray. Maybe Buddy can help too if it's to do with America.

North America.

OK, North America.

Now, here are statistics of the casualties in the war in Vietnam. We're supposed to say which war we think was more terrible.

I don't believe that, said Ray. Is that Mr Bligh again?

I most certainly don't want to hurry you folks, said

Buddy coming into the kitchen, but I found myself a plane and I gotta go, I really gotta go. You sure got a fancy telephone.

Look, I said. Don't get your plane. Not a plane. Come back with me on the train. I'd be . . . I'd be honoured if you did.

Hell. Pardon me.

And maybe you could help with this homework problem.

So long as it ain't Math or Biology, Buddy said.

It's your Civil War.

The ol' Stars and Bars.

Right, said Ned showing the page in his textbook, that's here in a picture.

Well all right!

It's the North American Civil War and Vietnam.

What's that supposed to mean, Vietnam?

The country, Vietnam.

Well OK.

Wait a minute, said Ray to Ned, your uncle Irwin will help you. Come on Buddy, let's drink tea, you're in England now.

Now wait a minute, I gotta see what it says here. What book is this? I never saw anything like this.

Come on, said Ray, forget it.

Hold on, said Buddy, the kid wants to do his homework.

See dad. Now look, the numbers of actual people killed were much worse than in the Civil War. But the fraction of people killed and hurt then was much worse.

You shouldn't be doing this at your age, Ray said. That's for university students.

So far, said Ned, I've put: 'The USA got involved in Vietnam in 1964. After almost ten years of war 56,000 US servicemen had been killed and 270,000 injured.' That's almost copied out straight. Now I have to say—

What do you mean? said Buddy angrily. What do you mean, 1964? You can see the future?

Future?

Caroline appeared with her purse.

I'm never going to put money in here, she said. I want it to smell like this always.

When I get back, said Buddy crouching down to her, you know what I'm going to make you? I'm going to make you a belt. And on this belt, round the back of this belt, where you're gonna back-belt it, it's gonna have your name on it, Caroline.

Caroline skipped away with her purse to the living room.

Dad, complained Ned, I'm not getting anywhere with this.

I'm going to call Mr Bligh and put an end to this nonsense. Veronica, do you have Mr Bligh's home number?

No! called Veronica from the living room.

So drop your homework Ned, I said. Take in some plates. Caroline, will you take in this packet of biscuits. Where's Caroline? Caroline! Please take in this packet of biscuits.

All right, I will.

Caroline put the biscuits against one ear and the purse against the other and followed Ned out.

We three men stood round the marguerites in the vase. I stood holding the tray. Buddy and Ray faced each other holding the backs of two chairs.

OK, said Buddy. What date is it? What year is it?

1999.

Boy. Oh boy.

It's true.

It can't be true.

It's true.

If it *was* true, how could I be here? I'd be sixty years old. You won't be here.

I won't be here. You guys are not OK.

Let's have the tea. We'll get this sorted out somehow.

Well how? You mean . . . are you from that bunch I read about up in New Hampshire, what the heck do they call themselves? . . . you're saying you know what's coming, you sayin' that . . . how'd that book get here, where'd it come from? . . . you mean . . . what do you mean? . . . you mean I get to go into this . . . war and I get killed. Is that what you cuckoos have to tell me?

No Buddy. That won't happen. It's OK.

It's OK, it's OK. It's crazy as hell and you keep saying it's OK.

Come on, let's go into the living room.

I am not going anywhere with you guys. I gotta get out of here. I'm gonna find a plane and get out of here.

Don't do that, Buddy. Stay with us. We'll get this sorted out.

The hell we will.

Buddy.

I'm going. I'm getting my things and I'm going. Next time you look my way I'll be gone.

I draped my coat, bag, my thoughts across the Virgin table and the neighbouring seats. Buddy was gone and the world was emptier without a celebrity in the air, a harder place to think straight in. I thought what I thought. Nothing earth-shaking. I was not working on a cure for Aids or a blueprint to combat poverty. While the Virgin train was approaching London, I was thinking, other trains were doing the same.

Converging trains. Almost converging: it wasn't as if every buffer finally touched, meeting at the heart of a star.

I tried more simple looking out of the window. I saw more station platforms and Anglia car parks all in their discoloured twilight look. I thought of the big planes stacked in their queues in the sky, while the Tube ran under and above its crossing selves, while the buses jammed against the cars. In the heart of the city, its stone-packed heart, people on foot cut great ragged streams, pigeons flapped back and forth, cyclists proceeded by stealth with tails of pretty red lights.

I could see Ned holding his school book; Caroline with her purse at her mouth.

The dark sky, thick from its endless night in space, was pushed aside by green, red, pink and orange shows of lights. The train negotiated a turnstile of points and high-voltage transformers. The closer into the city the more its lights crowded. Lights from cars jabbing and flashing. Floodlit parks and works idle at night. I sought to get a mental grip on all these lights, summing their effect by visualising a score of music with the bars put roughly on top of one another. I had this stack turn into a cylinder, I was thinking of pianolas and I had it play. The tune was a cacophony, the opposite of Buddy Holly, but I knew what I was doing. It was my sketch of the city from train-carriage level.

Approaching Liverpool Street the Virgin train passed other outgoing Virgin trains as other passengers left accompanied by Elvis, Janis, Jimi, John Lennon. Freddie Mercury. Kurt Cobain, Ian Curtis. By more intimate, private souls. The train approached the platform. The carriages gently halted. In the city, somewhere, songs by every recorded band and singer were being heard. Smoking traces of whatever had just happened waited to be discovered or obliterated. Tube trains carrying thousands intersected. At this hour the planes in the airport approaches were stacked so thick they could see one another in fours and fives. Hell, their passengers could almost count each other's windows as they circled in the sky.

BUTLEY

I ALWAYS WANTED to do it in the middle of nowhere.
Although there is no middle of nowhere. In these faraway fields of Suffolk you've still got a cow ambling across
to see what's going on, a dog on the loose, or a walker
springs out of nowhere. I know. I was that walker, out with
binoculars. In one yard of ground I went from focusing at a
marsh harrier flapping over brackish meadows to almost
treading on a young woman's ankles.

I'm talking about a grass bank about the size of a
blanket, which is what they had, beside the Butley River.
Which drains into the River Ore, into the North Sea. That's
just for orientation's sake. That's all there was. A few trees,
saltmarsh, bit of wind. The sky was vast, the clouds edging
over in white corrugations. There was a long hill I'd just
loped down, apparently an Anglo-Saxon mound. Mound of
what, my booklet didn't say. You could just see a line of sea
from its top. The white smidge of a ship on the horizon.
There were brown cows on the mound, but for their tails
all bulk and brawn. They started towards me, debating
whether to work up speed, but by then I'd got to the stile.
No people for a mile on this side of the Butley River, not
now. Long ago, my information said, the area had been
criss-crossed by a Queen of France. Moving to the present
moment: Lying near the blanket was a fresh fence-post
waiting to be put up, sharp at the end like a monster-sized
pencil. They were a quiet couple; no sound carried from
them. Water being blown downriver made a gulping sound
against two boats tied up in midstream. A rubber boot was

stuck on a pole where a ferry was supposed to row people over, only no ferry-boat was in sight. A couple of dinghies were upside down in mud. Towards the Ore was a boat moored to a rackety pier, its hull an acid green. That was it. Samphire in tufts on the banks, if you want to get colourful. Summing up, it was just one of those Suffolk places: a Queen of France, Anglo-Saxon mound, monster-pencil kind of place.

I—I—I'm so sorry, I was just walking. I could have added: to see the old priory and the oaks at Staverton Thicks. Where the Queen of France was supposed to have picnicked with monks. But it wasn't the moment for a conversation with details.

She decided to collapse face down into the blanket. He sat up with his T-shirt in his lap. She had a great pyramid of frizzy blonde hair. Concentrating on not looking where I shouldn't, I glimpsed a strong calf, a small tattoo.

He stood, more quickly in tune with the situation. Although he covered most of himself nimbly, I glimpsed he was carrying extra weight. He had something George Clooney about him, if you know George Clooney. It was partly his eyes, a wide-eyed seductiveness. At the initial contact, eyes were dominant in our actions. Face still to the ground, she groaned and opened hers. What the fuck, she said.

Looking away studiously, I caught the mid-summer light picking out ragwort (which, thinking about the middle of nowhere, would have been absent in Anglo-Saxon and Queen-of-France times) and a few poppies on the land side of the dike. I couldn't hurry off, I was too close to simply go.

Just walking? said George Clooney pulling up his shorts and eyeing my binoculars. It be a fair day for a walk. Come on, Suzie, he said offering to pull her up.

I watch birds, I replied, I was on a walk on the heath path and past the priory. In a split second of hip curve, nipple dark, collar bone, nose stud, Suzie stood; coolly and matter-of-factly, a courier on the doorstep waiting for a parcel to be signed for. I kept my eyes on her eyes, looking at most at the stud or the great volume of hair. She gave me a stormy I-cannot-wait-for-US-gun-laws-to-apply-here-too look.

The Queen of France was down here once, I said groping for something to say. No doubt you be meaning the Duchess of Suffolk, said George covering Suzie with his sweater. You been reading a guidebook too many, he added, because when she was Queen of France she was in France all the time. Then she stopped being Queen of France and come back. Maybe she did go to the woods with a monk or two, have an oyster from the beds up there, who knows. All gone now: she and the monks and the woods too. Oyster are still here, I suppose.

He kept holding out her sweater. She took it from him and pulled it on. During which she looked past me, in a glare part ice and part fire, I couldn't decide.

You made that up Ron, she said thrusting on her jeans. Except for the monks, maybe.

I didn't, he said shrugging, starting to fold the blanket.

I'd like to have been a queen, she said.

I bet, he said. You a king? he said turning to me. No? You know we're all in line for the throne.

I'd do just as I liked, she said pulling down the sweater. Twisting kings and courtiers around my fingers. Ah, said Ron, it's not like that: better to get someone with a boat. He's right, I ventured; look at Elizabeth, that isn't much of a life. Right, he said, and when she do what she want she just get in everybody's bad books.

The pace of dressing accelerated. Suzie fastened her jeans buttons. All dressed, we stood about the blanket in the middle of nowhere. Nowhere is a relative term, I'd decided. Getting used to nowhere was like getting used to the dark. Getting accustomed to it I saw there were people, birds, samphire, cows, dikes, oysters, auras of queens. Now the birds sang louder. A frog hopped in the grass.

Nice spot, I said.

Air's good, said Ron.

Some of the cows began mooing.

See that there, he said pointing to the mound: Burrow Hill. It used to be an island, now it's a hill. In a few years it'll be back under water.

You're from round here?

Sort of. Well. Care for a drink?

I saw no bottles, cans, rucksacks, nothing. I got a bar just down there, he said pointing to the acid-green boat, his boat: the nearest bar for miles.

I'm going the other way, I said, to see the oyster beds. We could come with you, eh Suzie. WALKER DISCOVERED FACE DOWN IN OYSTER BEDS. Yes Ronald, said Suzie standing on the path where the low dike ran; holding up a pair of sandals, ready to walk barefoot. What's *your* name? she asked. Callum, I said improvising. That Scottish or what? said Suzie. Scottish, I said. You don't talk Scottish, she said poking the boot on the post; I wonder how long that old boot's been here.

I fancy a stroll, said Ronald. We were out to get some exercise anyway.

We had only gone a few steps on the dike when Suzie stopped and turned. We won't get there from here, she said; the path ends and there's no way across.

It's worse than the Styx, said Ronald, if I got my rivers

65

right. They don't do that ferry any more. The last owner of it got run over by a truck. Them that work ferries often come to no good.

He looked at the sky.

It's that kind of a place, he said. You'll see when the water goes out. There be more than just oysters lying in them beds.

We could cross in the boat, Suzie said.

Yeah, said Ronald turning about. Have a beer first. This way, he insisted, after you.

I turned. It should be said: it was a lovely Suffolk day for a walk. All life seemed to appreciate being alive under that wide-angled sky. The cows were edging onto new grass. Buntings flitted from reed to reed on ahead. Red admirals made their mazy dithering trails.

Boyton Dock, they call that pair of posts I moored at, said Ronald. Look at them. A dock.

If that's a dock, said Suzie, I'm the Queen of Sheba, the Queen of France.

I know more about her than you'd be crediting me with, said Ronald. She were queen three months, from October to the first of January. I forget the year. He wore her out, then died. Just as well.

I should be so lucky, Suzie said.

Well that weren't the end of it. She come back to Suffolk and married that Charles Brandon of hers.

Anyway, said Suzie, that's all history. She's just an old queen.

History is just the same as now, he said. Only difference is the people are dead.

You're interested in local history? I said hesitantly. I was unable to shake off a helpless feeling, like a lost boy scout.

Am I? If I am I'm the original amateur. And you scoffing

like that, said Ronald turning on Suzie, it won't get you nowhere. You take an interest more and it'll stop you being like a keg of gunpowder all day.

Oh Ron, shut it.

No one is just some old queen. Are they Callum?

No.

You not a talker?

I—I can be, I said wondering about the nose stud and tattoo. So not an—I gave Ronald my best interested, enquiring look—an old dead queen?

Back home to Brandon she came, he said, and went on her picnics. She was marrying like in Hollywood. Divorcing Louis-something in January. Marrying Brandon in March. A regular politician, she knew how to go about things. Short on words and long on action. *Talking* about doing the will of God, then getting straight on with her parties and pleasure. But she also go into Blythburgh church on her own so she could talk to the angels in the roof. The bright angels. That's a fact. Several facts. How do you know? said Suzie stopping on one leg to look at the earth on her soles. I know, said Ronald touching his nose; mind your head when you come down here. Go careful, don't rock the boat, you already have once. Becks or Adnams? Becks is cold.

I do believe we be sat fast on the mud, said Ronald as the boat creaked but failed to move. Stuck in the mud with the tide up and all, he said scratching his chest. We sat in a horseshoe around a folding table at the stern. Our little mobile home, you might say, he declared. Enough room for two in the day but not much to sleep in. Is there a place to stay the night down there? he said pointing to a copse in the distance. You're local, I'm not, I said. We can walk to that Capel place, said Suzie; if there's nothing there, get a taxi to Orford. And then? said Ronald. A bus to Woodbridge, said Suzie still without a smile.

I like Woodbridge, I said. Orford.

Woodbridge, said Suzie. Yeah yeah yeah.

I can guess what you're thinking, Ronald said to me. How come I got this boat—I got it because I made money on the stock market. Lots of luck and lots of skill. You'd never credit how much money there is to be made in carpets. Potash. Vacuum cleaners. Things people need.

That sounded right. Ronald had a feeling of the local boy who'd made money but stayed local. Who used to open his beer bottles with a cigarette lighter and still would occasionally.

But where were we? he said.

Then to Woodbridge, said Suzie. Buy the usual sack of potash. Then we can take up where we were so rudely interrupted.

She disappeared through the curtain of dark beads at the little cabin doorway.

Not rudely, I objected. But I must apologise. I was just on a walk. Oh yes, said Ronald, the old Suffolk Coast and Heaths Path. But that don't pass the priory. No, I said, but I passed it. The adventurous sort are you, Curran? said Ronald drawing a smirk from Miss Suzie as she held the beads to one side. Shall I heat up that chilli? she said. Fine, said Ronald, you do that. There's no action on an empty stomach.

I mean, what have you done that's really adventurous? Bottle OK? You will have a little chilli, won't you? Con carne, as they say in Torremolinos. Do you want a glass, queen Suzie? Here. So, you were saying how you parachuted into a volcano, Curran. Callum.

That's right, I said cottoning on, only the wind carried me out to sea. Was you covered in ash? Ronald asked.

Oh the ash, the ash, I said. My mouth was full of it; on the next jump I carried a vacuum cleaner to make it easier for myself.

Wait, said Ronald wiping froth from his lip, you did no such thing. And we don't want to be made fun of, the queen and I.

I gatecrashed a party once, I ventured.

More than once I'd say, said Suzie reappearing to sip her beer.

Not any old party, a big fancy occasion.

And this isn't? said Ronald. Chilli and a cold beer on a warm day on the old Butley River. Extra information in terms of local history from yours truly. Not that we're in this life to gather information.

We're here to have a good time, said Suzie. Or try to.

Sh, Ronald interrupted.

Kee-yoo. Kyi-yi-yi-yi.

Ronald and I scoured the sky towards Orford.

It's that marsh harrier, he said.

I saw it. Before.

That used to be a rare bird in these parts, said Ronald. In most any parts. It live most likely on Orford Ness.

That's information too, I said.

You not taking me seriously? said Ronald. I should, if I was you I should.

It's just an old bird, said Suzie. Food's coming up.

Now I call that going to the opposite extreme, said Ronald. Just an old bird. Just an old river. The worn boredom, the tediousness of it all. I don't go for that.

How come this is a river anyway? said Suzie emerging through the beads with bowls. I thought a river has to go to the sea, or it's not a river.

It can go into another river that goes into the sea, replied

Ronald. So don't start calling it a backwater. Just an old backwater. We can stay in this boat and when the tide come for us we can get straight to Poland.

Suzie let three tin spoons drop on the table.

I'm not saying it'll never dry up, not one day. Like Minsmere almost has. Minsmere Old River, they say now.

See? said Suzie. An old river.

I'm a river person, Callum.

Oh yeah? said Suzie handing out bowls. Aquarius?

Don't give me that. I'm just saying chugging up and down rivers is my style. Away from the roads and the noise, the complications. I like to be in touch with how things have been for a long time. Apart from the boat itself of course, that won't have been here with the monks and the queens. The duchess.

Well aren't you the conversation stopper? said Suzie now kissing him on the forehead.

Did you put in the arsenic like I said? We can't have you smouldering with resentment all day.

Of course I put it in. I hope I got these bowls round the right way.

I can't taste it in mine, said Ronald. It don't have the tang.

You're not meant to taste it, said Suzie. How's yours?

OK. It's—it's good.

I made it myself. From scratch.

You mean you raised the cow, killed it, said Ronald. All in your spare time. Shinned the best part off the bone.

Yeah, said Suzie. I had my old stun gun ready.

I'm happy with it, said Ronald.

Me too, I said.

How happy?

Happy.

70

Out of ten?

Mm. Seven, eight.

You Suzie?

Three. I was happier earlier on.

Yes, said Ronald. The message be coming through. So, Cullem, what will you do next? We're stuck here, we can't get off the bottom to go and see the oyster beds. It gets too narrow that way anyway, we could wait for them cows to go home and we'd never get there, not from this side of the old river.

Old river? said Suzie. You said it again.

I was being affectionate.

I like that, said Suzie moving over to sit on his lap. I like it when you're being affectionate.

Any time now, Suzie. Mind my food. First just let the gentleman answer a question. What will you do?

I'll walk back the way I came.

Back to civilisation.

Suzie leaned away to look at Ronald. If I'd known how remote it is, she began. If we didn't have a phone we'd be as good as cut off.

We have got a phone, said Ronald.

Well I know. But strange things happen, like in the papers the whole time. Did you read that about a woman, a lady, standing on the street looking at the menu of a restaurant. The Casa Mastroianni.

You sure you got that name right?

She's reading the menu, thinking about macaroni cheese and *wham*, this car out of control launches her through the restaurant window. All because a 79-year-old at the wheel had a heart attack. Head wound and broken legs.

Jesus. And no macaroni. No parmesan.

You be serious with me too. I'm serious. I hadn't finished

about the cows either.

Where'd you read this then? said Ronald wiping his mouth with his hand.

It was an old paper lying about in that launderette.

It's a good tale, Suzie, said Ronald burping. If I wasn't chortling I'd be guffawing. You believe that? What about you Cullem, you believe that?

It's hard.

I just told you, said Suzie.

OK, I believe it, I said. Terrible. Just as well there aren't any restaurants out here.

Ronald burst out laughing. That is good Cullem, he said, that is good. Just when I was thinking you were sitting there nervously, tongue-tied I had you down for, and there you are all ready to shoot out the jokes.

Well, thanks for the food and drink, I'll be on my way.

Right you are. Suzie will follow with her stun gun.

Ronald, do you have to be so direct?

I was kidding. Callem will stay and have a cup of tea. Whatever else, I would wait until them cows go away. See them strolling, behind Burrow Hill? I know they look harmless. I expect I do. Even if Suzie don't. From here they look harmless, don't they?

Sort of, I said. They're not cuddly.

Not cuddly. You are a one, Caledonian: not cuddly. Not scared of cows, are you? Not got boviphobia? They sense that, they say. Like sharks smelling blood.

Boviphobia? said Suzie. Ron, you made that up. Like I keep wanting to say though, if I could get a word in, there was a story about cows in this paper too.

What paper is this? said Ronald.

Some paper. It was in the launderette, I just said. "Man crushed to death by cow", said Suzie. He went into a field of cows to light a bonfire—

That don't make sense.

It said that, said Suzie.

I'll put the kettle on, said Ronald getting up to rustle through the beads.

The paper said it looked like he'd been butted from behind.

How can they know? called Ronald from his galley.

Search me.

Milk, Cullum? We got milk from that cow of yours, Suze, the one we just been eating off? Lucky you didn't get crushed milking it.

That cow and I got on fine, called Suzie so Ronald could hear. You know how I am with beasts, you're a beast sometimes. I didn't go lighting bonfires beside it like that man in the paper.

I'll tell you one thing Suzie. I don't ever want to be "the man in the paper". How about you, Callum?

No thanks.

One day you're walking along, minding your own business—

Or not even doing that, said Suzie.

Then *bang*, you wake up reading about yourself in the papers. If you wake up at all.

Exactly, said Suzie getting excited.

What's got into you, Suze? All this reading the papers. Here we are, he said brushing past the beads. The cups at least. Hold this mug, Caledonian.

You know me, Ron. That's all I do read. Stories, nice and short.

It's time I went, I said.

Please yourself, said Suzie, I was only offering a bit of entertainment. You going to get that tea today, Ron?

Sit down, Callum. You haven't had that tea yet.

Nothing wrong with a bit of entertainment. For you and Mr Birdwatcher.

I got up again.

Ronald held my arm. I *want* you to stay, he said. I'm going to get the tea, and when I reappear from the witches' den there you will still be here, OK? Good. Now, Suzie. You didn't finish about the man with the bonfire, if I'm recapitulating right.

Didn't I?

She slapped Ronald's leg as he passed her.

You've been distracting me, Ron. You are so *evil*.

Evil is as evil do, eh Callum? Ronald called.

I smiled weakly.

Sometimes I get so pissed off at him, Colin, said Suzie, I want to squirt the calor gas at him and ask him for a light.

I heard that, said Ronald. But you don't smoke no more. I'd see through that.

It was just an example, Ron. I'm trickier than that.

Yeah, everybody's tricky when they're angry. What do you think, Callum?

The chilli was good.

Wait a minute, said Ronald holding back the beads. I asked a question.

Look, I really am so sorry I interrupted you back there.

That is forgotten, said Ronald. Buried and forgotten.

Buried, said Suzie. Halfway. Up to the neck.

I wondered what it was that was troubling you, he said. Keeping you quiet. Giving you the chills, maybe. Have some more chilli.

I will.

There isn't any, said Suzie.

That is comical, queen Suzie, called Ronald from the

other side of the curtain. Suzie in Wonderland.

The paper said, resumed Suzie, it looked like a cow had stepped on his arm while he was on the ground. Broken his wristwatch.

Lovely, called Ronald coming out with a teapot. Are you taking all this in, Callum? You got a wristwatch?

No.

Me neither. Trampled and stamped on by a cow, he said ducking back into the cabin, well I never.

But I've saved the best till last.

You would, wouldn't you, said Ronald holding the beads about his shoulders. You are the real beast around here, what with that in your nose. Go on then.

A fracture to the Adam's apple.

Ooh, I feel it, said Ronald holding his.

Course I don't have one of them, do I.

Be glad. You know that reminds me of something. Some film where somebody steps on somebody's head. It was out in the middle of nowhere.

Quite, I said.

Quite? Where is the milk then, Suze? We've had a lot of talk and no milk.

I don't know. Look for yourself.

I was. You come and look.

OK, if I must. Don't go away, Colin. I'll be right back.

She smiled as she made her way past. I was left to myself with the folding table and a dancing red butterfly. The rotting posts among the samphire.

I stood up, wondering which way the next bend of the river turned. If I could walk back a different way. Towards the Ore the dike seemed to flatten to nothing.

Hey Ron stop that, I heard Suzie saying. Ro-on, what are you doing?

They went quiet. I thought I heard the marsh harrier and whipped out my binoculars. It flapped and dipped in front of the copse.

On the verge of alerting them, I checked myself.

Behind the curtain were squeals and words in snatches.

Still the boat didn't rock when I moved. I managed to step quietly to land.

I walked quickly to the post with the boot. Over the stile and up Burrow Hill. Only then did I look back and saw there were no figures, no one waving or coming, no shouting. There were more ships on the horizon. A helicopter was coming in fast off the sea, getting louder. A remote corner of Suffolk had ceased being nowhere.

Turning away from the Butley I hastened down the mound, relieved to have behind me the incident, the boat and the chilli. Looking up at the sky, I found comfort, security, in the patterns of the clouds. I rejoined the Coast and Heaths Path, to arrive at the field with the cows. As happened when I came upon the strangers, I saw them seconds before they saw me.

STOUR

There was to Constable something overwhelming in the fact that Gainsborough had once walked the lanes that he now strolled in his slow, deliberate, country fashion. He saw Gainsborough 'in every hedge and hollow tree'.
— RONALD BLYTHE

WE ARE CREW. Easy to identify by the word in white-on-blue T-shirts. CREW sailing nowhere, constructing nothing, without ship, rum, bunks or mutinies, but with freight of a kind: attending to tourists of Constable country on a summer's day. My co-workers Patrick, Josh and Ant supply the nourishment to keep those tourists touring, and we have rowing boats for hire. Taking no shit, CREW can both knuckle down and party. Co-worker Patrick says the world is our accordion, our squeeze box. Josh, who's as digital as they come, compares a shift in CREW favourably to an Xbox gaming session. Ant doesn't talk; Ant *does*. That's him coaxing an Alsatian out of a rowing boat. We know what we are doing. We've seen it all before; we believe so.

Down at the Stour everyone stands in front of us sooner or later. Men and women fancying a performance at the rowlocks or having their fingers trail dreamily in the water; picnickers with a baby or a bottle of wine, children, the occasional birdwatcher or rambler—all draw near The Hut and drift off and some time loop back again, as if on an invisible length of elastic. They may have come to see where the Hay Wain was painted but what they *need* is a Magnum Classic or something chilled or even a beaker of what—co-worker Patrick says—we with a smile call coffee. As CREW on top of every situation we even have sun hats, camera batteries, sticking plaster—besides always having something quenching, says Josh, a bite or two. Something to lick, says Patrick.

Before they appear between our counter and the horse chestnut hanging in its plentiful cascades down over everything like hair in front of your eyes, I've mostly seen them already: today it's the family that gingerly stepped into a boat a half hour earlier, the raucous office outing, children paddling in the gravel shallows, the absorbed couple with him bare-chested and her in a skirt and bikini, back from a patch of grass among the buttercups in the water meadows, or those two nymphs that have been larking about today and will want something fizzy but I bet don't have a sou. But I won't be subsidising the nymphs, or waiving the costs if a constable—tricky word around here—a constable of the constabulary kind comes looking for a cup of tea. Shelley who regularly jumps off Dedham bridge is the only person to get free CREW treatment. We admire her for daring to let go of the railings and jump. Her feet touch the bottom and her knees bend, though the police say the danger is not to her but to river traffic. Traffic on the weir side of the bridge? Try portaging a rowing boat: one canoe a week goes that way.

Co-worker Howie? Have we got plenty of creamers?

We do, I tell co-worker Patrick.

We have no captain, no officers, mates or oilers.

Having forsaken the picnic benches where they've been failing to sit still for a moment—her in the pale doll's dress with her legs flopping apart so her raspberry knickers show, her friend in blue shorts with a knee up to a chin to better inspect her toenails—the nymphs are in the queue. She in the dress that keeps riding up is carrying nothing but a big black hairbrush; while at the most her good-looking friend has a banknote in her shorts but I doubt it. There's a lot of picking at the brush. A lot of zany inter-nymph talk from the doll to the shorts. Like:

Lorraine, did you and I have to meet—yes or no?

Not replying, Lorraine turns to me with her good looks, her blonde ringlets, white teeth and blue eyes, brown elbows on the counter.

Two Cokes.

No Cokes, ladies.

That's what we want.

Are you saying you don't have what we want? says the doll.

That's right.

For once I look on, not brushing the air, letting The Hut flies maraud the packets of sugar.

Such a good looking Mr Crew don't you think Maddy, says Lorraine. He could be spending time with me. He could be manning my ship. Two Pepsis.

Instead of replying I pretend to chew gum.

The doll Maddy points her brush at me. It feels threat-ening not like a gun but indeed like a brush, as if it had slurping black paint ready to daub. Come on Lorraine, she says.

Not before I kiss this counter, says Lorraine.

They giggle as she does. The doll stops to look back sternly over her shoulder: We'll be back.

What was that about, Howie?

No money. I can tell. CREW instinct.

Against the panorama of buttercups a green Mad River Canoe with two men in baseball caps glides by. From the opposite direction a rowing boat drifts into sight with a girl in white face-down, draping and shaping herself into its bows, fingers in the water.

I'm dripping, says big Shelley with her green T-shirt darkening the space before me. Did you see me jump?

Nope. Can't see the bridge from The Hut, only a tree. If I lean across the counter—I demonstrate while watching out for the nymphs—I can just see the meadows the other way towards Flatford. That's all.

The girl in white in the boat lifts her head to try stretching both arms to the side like on the *Titanic*.

The police thought they had me but I got out on the Suffolk side, says Shelley with her black hair swiping Stour water on the counter. They were from Essex. They nearly always are.

The parking's easier on the Essex side.

Exactly. Parking's easier in Essex. Swimming's better in Suffolk. I saw a snake swim from the Essex bank to the Suffolk the other day. Hi Patrick.

Hi Shell. You just come over from Suffolk? Is Flatford Mill in Essex or Suffolk?

Not a clue. Who cares? I'm where the action is now. Don't tell me it's Constable country, it's Shell-shire.

Your jumping is a modern-day miracle, says Patrick. A galvaniser.

Too true. Have you seen those two girls? When they saw what I was doing it stopped them wittering. Stopped them in their tracks.

Howie saw them. Briefly. Dealt with them like a hero. One had eyes that would melt most men, but not CREW. How'd you resist, co-worker Howie?

No idea, co-worker Patrick. You want a drink Shell?

No thanks.

What will you do now?

Dry off. Hang around.

Need a towel? says Josh appearing behind her.

Nah. Bye, you two. Bye Josh.

Time CREW swung into action too, says Patrick. Better stock up on the cold, cold stuff. We're doing fine on tea, aren't we? I reckon we sell one tea an hour. Tea is on the way out altogether. Like they used to have snuff and now you don't. Wigs. Like people used to go skying and now they don't.

What's that?

You make it easy for me to say, co-worker Howie. Skying means recording the moods of the sky.

What's it to be? Two blueberry muffins. Change? CREW always has change. Why do that?

Skying? Constable did.

Would he do it now?

Good point. I'll be back with a possible answer.

Next. Wanting a boat come the bare-chested possibly office worker, possibly wannabe internet tycoon, with a starlet in a yellow bikini. Twenty-pound note. A contrast in looks and in skins. He has a rash on his back he can't see while her skin, lightly browning, is spectacularly unblemished. What a mismatch. Unless she's a fluffhead. Could be. I watch them on the walkway. He pushes back his shoulders to show her what it might look like when she takes to the oars in her bikini. She tells him not to rock the boat so he promises he won't and then he does. Nothing new under the stars, says Patrick returning.

We're new, I insist.

The starlet somehow gets straight back out of the boat. Bare-chested docks and clambers out after her. CREW hold the rope. She stops conveniently right in front of The Hut and he shouts at her *You fucking cow you wouldn't know a bit of fun if it come up and hit you like a rake.* As he shouts she resolutely takes from him the bag with their belongings.

When he pauses and begins a new sentence she stands back to improve her balance and with perfect delivery slaps him in the face. A good fifty people turn to see where this almighty crack has come from. The Hut flies freeze. In the distance a line of cows look up. She turns crisply and heads for the car park. Flies that stopped in mid-air resume flying. Meanwhile he of the red face, red head, having staggered, having lost it, stands with his head amongst the horse chestnut, stomach interrupting the view of the meadow, in shock. This reeks of a challenge; nothing on the shelves has prepared CREW for this. In no time she returns in shoes, blouse and a skirt. Keeping a safe distance from bare-chested she dangles a bunch of keys.

I think this is called playing to the audience, comments co-worker Patrick.

Turning her back to The Hut she throws the keys awkwardly overarm into the Stour.

Out of practice, says Patrick drily.

Ex-bikini departs brusquely. Shelley dives in. Lorraine and Maddy finally settle at a picnic table, subdued, acknowledging they will never now be today's centre of attention. I trade places with Josh at the boats. While waiting with a towel for Shell I take in the panorama of the meadows and the line of old dry willows posted along the river bank, with their split trunks and branches fanning in spokes. I always enjoy this sight but it is never in full view from The Hut. Miraculous Shelley surfaces, sleek black hair and dripping water, tosses the keys onto the walkway before bobbing under and swimming the few yards over to Suffolk. Clapping starts and dies immediately. Patrick offers bare-chested an XL CREW T-shirt in a blue paler than the usual shirts. Constables arrive, from Essex. The constables and ex-bare-chested, now in a sense also CREW, walk away together,

82

leaving me with the meadow and the willows. Shelley, now big with blotchy white legs, waves from the bank. We would be delighted to have her as CREW if she wanted, but she doesn't. To shed a weight of water from her hair she shakes her head like an animal before walking towards the bridge. As if to complete the panorama of buttercups again, the Mad River Canoe with the baseball caps glides back by. Sunlight flashes at the water splashing from a paddle. CREW together with Shell could not have done more. Pearl-diving apart, we can do anything. Patrick goes over to the two dippy girls as I turn my attention to the meadow, seizing that moment to look to the sky.

PARRETT

M IXED MARRIAGES MAY be prone to being doomed,
but this wisdom has failed to sway our family. We
boldly marry across borders; any one of us is likely to be
half of this, quarter of that, one thirty-second Welsh and so
on. Across the world we stretch, for it seems we gladly live
elsewhere too. There are Parretts in New Zealand, most of
them now called Downie, the de Ryckes in Tournai, even a
Parrett now a Tang last heard of in Shanghai. Tracing along
the family tree we have a branch that grew but died out in
that Spanish town I forget the name of. Move to the present
and there is Hanski happily trapping insects in Namibia,
while Leo has become a Mehta in all but name. One branch
alone dwelt in Somerset by the River Parrett, which now
has a single representative in distance of its watery reeds
and eels and wading whimbrels: myself.

*Father said he would put his kettle on—last year, when he was for-
ever in that brown dressing gown. Shuffling to the kitchen he picked
up the phone. Put it down. Came back and sat down; wondered why
no water boiled.*

Other family members are welcome to trace our ancestry
in their two-thousand-word bash (the absolute limit, Leo
says). I will simply add something personal, in my own
quiet fashion. Only now am I putting this into words. I will
be composing Three Loves (working title), my contribution
to the Parrett Family History, J. Parrett, in the little
upstairs room with the Quantocks in the distance; com-

84

posing as long as the cat isn't on the windowsill blocking the view, get *down*, no I won't stroke you, I'm in the middle of thinking. Love Number Three—why create a mystery where there isn't one?—was my father. *Four* including me, the cat—impertinent brown creature— points out by springing onto my thigh and performing its treading-on-the-spot routine with its *four* paws. *Ouch! And (claw)* it's high time you used a name with me, OK? says the cat treading at half-claw: using a name is a serious matter, *OK? Ow!* I'll use a name soon, I promise, now leave me to get on with this account of my *four* loves, vamoose. Off the cat gets, shoots down the stairs. Alone at last. As I was saying, now I'm putting this into words in the little upstairs room. Taking my time; mulling over events with the cat as I seek to recount matters in the Somerset way, without false flair or colour.

It began in Amsterdam. In that city built on mud. On air, some say, referring to the way the upper storeys of the houses lean across the street. As an ex-structural-engineer —perhaps a response to the genetic Parrett imperative to react to the presence of mud—I know the houses are built this way simply to lessen the strain on the walls. I digress; possibly on account of the proximity to mud and the family river—the River Parrett, Bridgwater, Westonzoyland. Finally, since I'm still clearing the way for myself (you can't imagine the piles of books and papers in this humble cot- tage of mine): I'll be putting everything down as it comes, mud on the page, and will clean it up later, or whatever it is writers do exactly with their accounts.

In his final days I saw father try to water a hibiscus from a jug he discovered was filled with milk.

85

Sensing I was thinking of milk the cat jumped into my lap, licked at my forearm with its dry tongue.

I was in the said city built on marsh and bog, the son of my dear father who left for work with a diplomatic briefcase, of a mother whose dreams began and ended at her family. As a kid with brothers and sisters ahead of me I made friends easily, which is how I met my first love, Elleke, like me aged six. She had the sweetest nose and spun-gold hair always in what our American cousins call a barrette.

Barrette—spelling? No use asking father now; he's gone. He was good at spelling. It seems I can't serve broccoli well—he said the day he emptied a saucepan of it on his head, when I found him on his knees beside the cooker—but I can spell it for you, try me. Back in his chair he spelled paraphernalia. Cirrhosis. Diarrhoea.

Elleke's knees were the brownest and her white socks left lovely ribbed marks when I pulled them down, a fabulous deed allowed me once. Imagine her name if she'd become a Parrett on the tree: Elleke Parrett. Not that kind of parrot, cat, Parrett, E-double-T, how many times do I have to tell you? Cat can't spell a thing. Whether the cat sat on the mat or mat on the cat is all the same to it. Please don't lick my hand while I'm typing. I'll leave the family trees to Leo, who thinks life is so long why not dawdle along photographing headstones, spend your young years chatting away to town clerks and rectors. Leo. Thinks he has all the time in the world: what a phrase.

The sky fell clattering on me when Elleke's parents let it be known they were leaving for another life in South America. I must have blubbed and blubbed into my pillow. Eventually my father came. I was still young enough to be able to tell him, sobs running down my throat, 'because Elleke . . . is going to live . . . so far away and will . . . never come back'. He went away thoughtfully. The next day he returned upbeat from his work, saying to me brightly:

I have the solution. *You are to become a pilot.*

Father father, one and only father.

As he was, before he began his dressing-gown life. Should I spell out what kind of father? Cat says don't bother, organise food on saucer instead. Enquire locally about getting pet mice.

There began my passion for aeroplanes and travel. At first with a box of tissues and an aching heart, I spent afternoons at Schiphol observation lounge. One day during my Schiphol phase mum almightily smashed a tray with glasses on the kitchen floor. I can't stand stand stand stand it, she screamed. Then go, dad said, anywhere, but go.

Coming closer to my bright dream of pilothood, dad and I flew in a Dakota to London for a week. Working my way to Elleke, I thought nothing of the wings shaking and rivets jumping the whole journey, all on a summer's day. In London dad said, 'We're all going to have a good time here, and that means you should shake the cobwebs out of your English.' He plonked me in front of a television. 'This is your TV, Jeremy, to watch every day for as long as you like.' Tiny and black-and-white as they were, with few programmes, TVs were a big deal in those days.

Back in Amsterdam, dad and I visited the old Fokker plant on Papaverweg. I held off every brother and sister to build a pair of Fokkers, followed by a handsome fleet of balsawood gliders, their noses squeezed by lead weights and with thick rubber bands for launchers. With the help of our larger family I had Airfix models imported from the UK and Revells from the United States. Life was oily-coloured plastic shapes, glue and decals. In no time I could tell planes apart the way other people can birds or flowers. As father later reminded me, I was sketching fantastic flying machines on huge sheets of paper you don't find easily nowadays, to fall asleep on crumpled masterpieces. *Elleke who?*

Father opened his door. To let the cat out, he said. He had no cat, it's me who has the cat. He looked up and down the lane. There's that bright star again, he said. Then he saw the stray. Here's the cat, he said. It's true it had the right brown tabby look. It wound itself round and round his legs. There you are kitty, he said, would you like some crunchy bits? In it came. He scratched his head and closed the door.

As I was glueing the final parts to a magnificent swan-white Sunderland flying boat, ready to show my dear father, he vanished to Portugal 'to look for a cousin lost at sea'. He was gone for months. Do all his affairs make him a monster? Cat looks one way then the other at invisible particles in the air and agrees they do not. Cats chase mice but are not monsters for it. Can Nazi sympathisers write great literature or are they just monsters? Cat says it does not know. Says: Is not a great reader (has never read anything as far as I know).

As the 1960s dawned we moved to Denmark. Denmark felt odd; it was not quite the place to be. Or perhaps *we were odd*. At least at the international school I was among people speaking English. They included, indeed were mainly, Sirpa Lerby. A typical Parrett attraction, towards a person of such a mélange—in her case Scandinavian. My second love.

To this day I'm not clear why Sirpa agreed to go for walks with me. My Dutch past made me different, she said, as if I had spent my childhood negotiating coffee prices with sea barons. She got on extraordinarily well with my father, who ever since he was in Portugal was getting on worse and worse with my mother. Who, in most unfatherly fashion, confided to me, 'Jeremy, you know, I'm still growing, growing.'

It was typical of father to unhesitatingly lend me his Vauxhall—the steering on the right. One weekend Sirpa Lerby and I set off, just we two, only to break down outside Copenhagen. I checked the spark plugs. When I took the silver paper from Sirpa's chocolate bar to enhance their conductivity, she turned the key and the engine started.

Study engineering, my father said.

Father father, I did. For years I advised mining concerns ... Note to self: add later if at all. Ditto hobbies. Bird-watching? suggests cat. How do you know I do that, cat? Seen me pointing binoculars at birds in the sky. Joke, listen: Walker comes across bird-watcher looking through tele-scope. Do you want to look? bird-watcher says, it's a hobby. I know, says the walker walking on. Cat asks what's funny about that. Because, I say, he doesn't know a hobby is a bird. Cat: grins.

As my studies were creeping to their conclusion I announced Sirpa Lerby and I were to marry. Fat in a white-hot pan, flying in dollops across the world to all the family members. Too young, too young, a great mistake—all but my father said. Why the hurry, why so fast? they quizzed him. He's my son, he replied.

So despite family misgivings, Sirpa Lerby did become Sirpa Parrett, and naturally she expressed a desire to see the river of her name. Out of this wish we fashioned the trip for our calamitous honeymoon. Off we went in the old Vauxhall, specially serviced. And once in England the steering on the right stopped being difficult and it drove naturally on the left, a triumph of foresight for which I hold dad responsible, bless his departed dressing-gowned soul. We saw old Harwich, staying at a lovely place my father recommended from his many restless travels. On we went to Oxford. To Lyme Regis, where we confused the beaches and looked in vain for fossils.

Note to self: should have earlier mentioned admiration for Brunel (Clifton suspension bridge, the Great Eastern!). Love that photograph of him in a top hat standing in front of those great chains smoking a cigar. Could frame a copy, set it over the mantelpiece. Have to make room somehow (stash Leonardos in shed with Picassos, cat says).

Given my interest in engineering it was no surprise I was on the trail of the great Victorian engineer, Isambard Kingdom Brunel. Sirpa in the meantime still yearned for a sight of the family river, the Parrett. From Lyme Regis, Brunel led west to Cornwall with his bridge across the Tamar, but the Parrett was due north.

It will be so lovely when we have children, said Sirpa in the little car park by the sea at Lyme.

What children? I said.

Our children, she said.

We don't have any.

We will. That's the point of marriage.

Not for me it isn't. I married to be with you, Sirp.

Me with YOU?

Etecetera. Louder and louder. She clenched her fists and pushed her arms down, like in a picture by that Dutch painter van der Lat (how I remember the reproductions in the childhood home, at the top of the stairs). Like pistons, to get the anger out.

Van der Lat isn't right. Beck? Lak? Where are those pictures, where to start looking. Why bother. Why, because disrespectful to misname a great artist. Little tale, relevant, listen. Tale of respect, of those that have come and gone, as father has.

Church caretaker praised for keeping graves clean—the best they've ever looked, people said. Don't like hearing that—he said—because there's other people did this job before me. (All dead themselves of course.) Caretaker nuts? How many lives have you had so far, tabby? Has sloped off not deigning to reply.

So Sirpa wanted kids and what did I want, no idea. She took her suitcase with the flower patterns out of the boot and stormed off up the Lyme Regis street. I sat in the car.

Cat returns to occupy armchair. If it were me, it seems to be saying as it licks a paw, I would have sat on a rooftop and waited for lovely firemen, made a big scene to embarrass you. I turn to look at the Quantocks. The cat cannot appreciate the sweet pain of nostalgia.

Lyme Regis: Sirpa was holing up somewhere. I reached for the phone. She too was phoning, apparently. Within hours we were known (not by my father, let me add) from Copenhagen to Dubai as Mr and Mrs Unreasonable. Knowing Sirpa as I do, however, I suspect she was also thinking of our newly appointed flat in Oehlenschlägersgade. The mound of presents.

We met by chance in a back street; drove homewards in silence seeing neither the Parrett nor the Tamar. But we made it up.

Misunderstandings happen, said my father at the time. The result of poor communication. You young people, he said employing locutions ahead of his time (their time), are supposed to *be into communication.*

Eventually I took courses in communications. Sirpa and I stayed together. We had our beautiful children, Hanski and Leo. We lasted a few years beyond. Later Sirpa fell to pieces, went back to Helsinki, not to be seen in years.

The cat scratches the armchair to gain attention. It says I may refer to it as a brown tabby—the result of the agouti gene, it adds displaying its knowledge of genetics—but I am to realise that tabby is not a cats' word and by permitting such terms to be used it is doing me and all humans a favour, had I got that straight? Cat pushes its nose onto mine: I am simply trying to help communication. Unlike your old dad, the cat goes on, who was not striving to communicate. Whoa, I say, he couldn't help it. Seeing my distress cat says: OK you mutt of a human. I look into those pale green eyes. Look, they say, I know you loved your dad but just don't break down; it's not in my interests. How about just two pet mice? Maybe we could get them on trial.

If Sirpa never got to see the Parrett, Hanski and Leo have. They came to see their grandfather and me last year, after I had moved back like father before me, two salmon up the river. We met in London and made the trip to Westonzoyland through the south. Leo spent an afternoon quizzing his dressing-gowned grandpa, seeing him for the last time; then passed rain-filled hours examining records and graves at Isle Abbots, Chedzoy, Westonzoyland.

Cat says Leo is a no-hoper. Better to stick to Hanski. Hanski stroked me a lot, it says back on the windowsill blocking out the Quantocks: I will only move away from the window if you write about Hanski. She understood my joy in pouncing, the brilliant engineering of my whiskers, even my secret French yearnings. Oh really? I say out loud, that's the first I've heard about them. Cat turns to me: she called me Poussiquette.

But look elsewhere in the Parrett Family History for Hanski's account of how she found the home country. Her trip initiated her in many things English, making a true Parrett of her as well.

Cat not satisfied. Jumps suddenly across to the armchair. Pounces at my headphones and starts boxing them until I have to intervene. I try holding it down on the armchair.

Settling in, cat gives me the slow, slow shutting of the eyes it uses to express how it knows everything so much better. A second blink expresses incredulity: I have neglected to say what happened when the Parretts saw the Parrett. Parrett with E, cat indicates by pulling its mouth wide. Cat says I may admire its handsome whiskers from a distance and closes its eyes. Purrs.

Having seen the Parrett, we returned to Westonzoyland. Purrs.

Well did you see whimbrels? father asked his grandchildren. What are whimbrels? Leo said. Don't you know?—birds.

Birds? Cat opens eyes.

This modest contribution is dedicated to Hanski and Leo. After I've cleaned it up it won't be a word over two thousand. Almost done. Clap hands.

Up jumps the cat. Parades across the keyboard. fvcn/j ppppppppppppp. Shows its bushy tail.

Could put the kettle on.

Miss him. The growing, growing father.

This is your TV. Be a pilot.

Cat licks my hand: now you have me. And—stops licking, stands all four legs on one thigh, briefly inserts claws in eyeball-to-eyeball stand-off—now that you know my name, kindly use it.

Jumps down, rubs itself along the bookshelf. Stretches at the top of the stairs, looks at me as I get up.

Poussiquette?

Cat shoots down the stairs. I follow.

KENNET

THINKING OF IT as a live funeral, we came in numbers. From across the country—Martin and Sally literally, for despite that June's uncertain skies they had hiked across from the Ridgeway. Hail, we said, hail—something we had probably not uttered before or since. We moved off taking water, rainwear, no one had thought to bring a torch. The face of David pale as paper beside Jenny, her hair re-grown into a stubble; Martin and Sally; Shirley Bates; Jenny's sister Beth and Randeep; Linda; a man called Cees from the Netherlands; Alexis with Tom; Moth and Jenny, how often had we said Moth and Jenny in one breath, how long would it be before we uncoupled their names entirely; Inner Tube and Caramonga (so the children called each other that day), Wenceslas the dog. We made a caravan of people from the layby, the last car door shutting—a loose string with Jenny and David now passing over the Kennet close to its source at the Swallowhead, the first of us turning into the grassy avenue mown beside a perfect field of still-green corn—to the frayed head of the line where Wenceslas repeatedly bounded, stopped and tore off, ready to pass right by West Kennet Long Barrow and cross the plateau of the Wiltshire Downs before tumbling down the Vale of Pewsey.

The string grew a knot at the foot of the broad track as Jenny conferred with David and all but Martin and Sally waited. Should she sit, be carried, wait, drink more, give up, glean the prospects from shifts made by the clouds, follow later? And David to her: should we wait, go on, go

95

back? Jenny sat up, tiny in her brown jacket against the still-green corn, tiny and shockingly thin; eyes red and bleary, cheeks sallow; David crouching in front of her, playing with a long stalk of feathery grass. Small birds dipped in and out of the corn. Warblers, buntings? Was no bird expert among us? Did we not have the resources for all, almost all situations? And for this?—situation, march, celebration; words had ceased to be adequate for anything. Come here you rascal, Randeep was saying to Caramonga, who was playing a thwarting game with Inner Tube and would not come here. Shirley Bates told Randeep his orange turban—marigold actually, Randeep corrected— made him look as if he was our leader. So why won't he do what I say? Randeep replied. In the distance, Martin signalled he and Sally were going on to the Long Barrow. Jenny sat with her legs out, legs thin as sticks. The shadow of a cloud raced down the hill across the grass. David, spinning away from Jenny for a moment, whispering to me: I tell you, I've got nothing left to give. With airs like a young professor Cees stood next to Linda—Linda now into digital photography, with a silver camera strapped to her wrist—listening with apparent intensity to Shirley Bates, who I understood was once Jenny's supervisor and now, in her heeled shoes and blue suit, looked more ready to take on a boardroom than a walk over turf.

At the far side of the track, where a strip of grasses grew, Alexis was in a seething row with Tom, something to do with kitchen improvements. Wenceslas barked impatiently and was chased by Inner Tube who kept pointing at every man, woman, child or dog with a rolled-up umbrella; Caramonga kept blocking her only to be shot by the umbrella and fall back in the stubble or—until Beth told him to stop for the sake of the butterflies—

tumble into the grasses across the way. He doesn't listen to anyone these days, she said to everyone; no I don't know what those birds are, she told me. They're not vultures, said Randeep. Still Jenny sat against the corn, its stiff stalks pushed permanently at an angle, as if in fear or awe of everything that came from across the hills to the south. Indeed ever-darkening series of clouds were approaching from the south-west, so that — Randeep pointed out — we might know the earth is still turning.

Throughout Moth was Moth, quiet as ever in her pale good looks, neither glad nor anxious to be standing apart. She stood in one spot folding and unfolding her newspaper, seemingly unconcerned at the welter of people and talk. As a cloud put our gathering in shadow I saw her unhurriedly fold her paper and walk across to Jenny. As if to undo the knot of people in one pull she put a firm hand in front of David and told Jenny she was sure she would make it to the Long Barrow somehow. Jenny duly got to her feet; we all moved into new space; the caravan continued.

In step alongside Moth, neither she nor I found words for a conversation. I dropped back, as it was easier to drop back than to walk faster, from Moth, back from Beth, from Shirley and Cees. David was relieved not to be alone with Jenny. No, Jenny was saying to Linda, you certainly won't be taking a photograph of me — can you keep that dog away I'm afraid it's going to jump up, whose dog is it anyway? Not mine, said Randeep, not technically so; Charlie and Debbie — Inner Tube and Caramonga — have joint ownership; I conferred it on them two Christmases ago. Christmas? Randeep? said Jenny.

Yes, said Randeep, get *down*. OK it's not a puppy any longer. However, it is the same animal. But like I said, it's not mine. Get yourself a lawyer if you want to take that any further. *Wenceslas, stop* that.

You too Inner Tube, said Charlie-Caramonga pointing at his sister with her umbrella. *Stop!* You just shot yourself in the foot.

No I didn't.

What was I saying? said Randeep.

And your bullet went straight through onto this path, said Charlie, which is four thousand, five hundred years old. Like the barrow.

What barrow? said his sister looking around everywhere.

West Kennet Long Barrow, WKLB. Where you used to go when you were dead.

So?

So?

So I'll shoot it up when I get there.

Hey, young lady, said Randeep. You'll have run out of ammunition by then.

Is the English countryside often like this? said Cees, so tall he bent down to speak. Often? said Randeep. With so few trees, said Cees, such a panorama. It's different, said Linda, I'm always taking pictures and it's different wherever you go. Can you be more specific? said Cees. In this part of Wiltshire, said Linda, it's very gentle and flowing. Hm, said Randeep, really. Yes really, said Linda, it all changes very gradually, the hills undulate ever so slowly, it's like going over a human body. If you were to stroke it it would remind you of the shapes of a human body. Hm, said Randeep again, I must loosen my tie.

I wonder if I'll ever see this again, said Jenny stumbling at a dip in the turf. Where is David? Somebody hold me a while, please. I will, said Cees, we're halfway already; look, you can see the stones. That's the entrance, said Shirley

Bates falling in with us—I've been here before but I swore never again, because people, hippies and new travellers or whatever they call themselves, leave their candles and tea lights and blacken the stones and turn it into such a mess for everyone. Don't add to my anticipation, said Jenny. Well I'm sorry, but you can only see the place as it is. It's like everywhere: leave people to do what they want and of course in no time you have to put a fence around it. The Stonehenge syndrome, I call it.

I like a good syndrome, said Randeep.

Shirley said nothing.

I caught up with Moth.

So? I said.

We slowed our steps; looked ahead.

She'll die soon, Moth said.

What's to be done?

Nobody knows.

Don't you want to be with Jenny?

I have been with Jenny.

Maybe she needs you.

Me? What she most needs—she can't have. It makes me angry. But I'm not angry today. I was angry. I may be again.

The worst, said Linda drawing alongside, is her having to go through this shit. The therapies. Radiotherapy, chemotherapy. Having to talk about how you're just skin and bone. The spots on your face. Things you never had to deal with, yesterday.

But who lives with yesterday? said Cees.

What does that mean? said Moth.

We've arrived, I said. This is the forecourt. These boulders are to cover the entrance.

Not any more, said Linda. There's the way in? Where is

Randeep? I need cheering up. Now the dog's inside, what's its name?

Wenceslas, I said, but don't ask me why. The whole family is a turmoil of names.

Not me, said Randeep. I'm Randeep. Always Randeep.

It's dark in there, said Moth. I'm going to sit on top and read the paper.

David, worn out: I can't take this any longer; it's destroying me too.

I'll be reading the paper.

Grass waved on top of the Long Barrow mound. Linda feverishly photographed the land to the south, checking the results in her viewer. Look, she said to Cees, the colours are just not right. See there, that should be charcoal, zinc, navy, and is it?—and you see that line of sky under everything, look for yourself, that should be a baby blue and here it's more turquoise. It's a good camera though, said Cees, isn't it, a Canon? I followed the baby blue around each point of the compass until I saw Alexis and Tom had returned to their car and were driving off—as if their own concerns mattered more. David told Jenny they had just texted her an apology. Is Alexis pregnant? said Jenny suddenly. Text her back from me and say 'Are you pregnant?'. David tussled with the phone. No, he said eventually; she says no. Who invited Shirley Bates? she asked David next. You did, he replied. But I haven't seen her for years. That's what you said, David replied, you said you hadn't seen her for years so why shouldn't she come along, and now she has; and now that's enough questions; I can't make everything turn out the way you want. Uh, said Jenny with disgust, you're no use. David on edge: Because I haven't got infinite patience, well who has? Jenny: I—leave me alone. I'm going in the chamber.

I'll come too, I said.

The entrance was dark. I turned to Jenny.

Can you manage?

Cold and wet, Jenny said. Sounds are different.

There's a light at the end. Glass blocks in the roof.

They found 46 bodies here, or parts of them.

It feels there are almost as many of us.

I invited 46, Jenny said.

You didn't.

Not really, no. Cold, she said hugging herself. What's that noise?

A helicopter. Overhead somewhere.

Wherever you go there's a helicopter, said Jenny. Figuratively speaking. Crashing the party. Remember birthday parties? They always wound out of control. Not—

Not?

Not that this is a birthday. More the opposite.

The sound died away.

Jenny shivered: It's chilly.

Shall we go back out?

Once I was at Highgate cemetery, said Jenny. Buried in a family crypt, I thought, I would still hear the rain. In this barrow I could imagine still hearing the rain on the stones above.

We can hope—

Like part would still be living—hearing; seeing. All passive things; just not being able to act. Feeling the long cold nights. That's what I imagine, or is it hope, do I hope. It's nonsense isn't it, all nonsense. Where is Moth?

She's reading the paper, I said pointing above our heads: on the mound.

The paper.

You'll see for yourself. Like she had a table in a café. The pages smoothed flat. A prehistoric barrow to herself.

Yes, sitting calmly, said Jenny. I bet not even the clouds will want to move across her. Moth is so beautiful. I can't believe that won't last for ever.

It's hard to believe—a lot of things.

Reading the serious pages, said Jenny. Moth. Changing the subject: David's exhausted. I've exhausted him. The situation has.

There you are, Jenny.

Hi, Randeep.

I almost lost my turban at the entrance. What is it they say?—there's always a price. But: let's see who's sorry when the rain comes down.

You'll get wet too, said Jenny. Rain is very democratic.

Indeed. Those banks of cloud are certainly banking though. You know that Cees knows the names of clouds in English, isn't that *amazing*. I can't tell a cirrus from a black hole. We have all been studying them. Your friend Linda with the camera gave us all sections of the sky to follow. Even Shirley Bates has been looking for holes in the sky to close. And they have closed. We should make a move back down. We could all get in here of course and hope, and pray, for the rain to go. But I think a car roof will make a greater impression on a rainstorm. Or a rainstorm less on a roof. No no, don't anybody quiz me. Shall I give you a hand?

Hello, Jenny, said Martin. You made it.

Oh yes, Jenny said, I made it. Where have you two been?

We were scouting ahead. See that track right in the distance? We'll be there in under an hour.

Aren't you staying with us?

We'll get wet whatever we do. And we have the clothes for it. We could go back with you but somehow it just doesn't appeal.

In that case, Jenny began.

Yes.

In that case goodbye.

Yes. Yes, goodbye. Goodbye, Jen.

Goodbye, Jen, said Sally. We'll—

Say it, said Jen.

I can't say it.

Miss you, said Martin. We'll miss you. Very sad.

Where's David? said Jenny starting to cry. I need David.

Here I am.

We better go back. We're going to get wet.

Or stay here.

No.

Tell—

Who?

I don't know, said Jenny sobbing. I don't know who. I don't even know what I wanted to say. Look at this stone, it's lovely. It's so smooth.

Swoops and scoops, said Beth touching it.

Swoops and scoops, Debbie Inner Tube repeated. It's all black here. It's on my fingers.

The tea lights. Candles.

Don't everybody look at me, said Randeep with his hands up. Whatever I'm doing, I never use candles. Never. Quote me.

Tea lights? said Jenny. What for?

You know—rituals, like Shirley was saying.

Where is Shirley?

Here I am.

Where's Moth?

Here.

I guess we're all here then, said Jenny. Gathered. What a

meeting place. I'd never have got all 46 in here. Now we're all here I'm going to cry.

And a dog, Charlie added. He's trying to make a bed with that bit of old straw. Why is everyone crying?

David: Let's go.

The open air was dark.

How about a picture now, said Cees.

You're joking, said Linda. It will rain any moment.

Shirley? said Jenny.

Yes.

You've stopped work now?

Long ago. Though since you left, even then, it was never the same. You made such a difference, Jenny.

Thanks. There was a question I wanted to put to you, but now I don't know what the question is.

Ask away. I've been asked all kinds of things.

I can't say. That's all.

Where's that umbrella? said Randeep. Come here rascal number two.

I'm number one, said Debbie Inner Tube. Here, if you must have it.

Thank you number one. Now let's get you under here. Age before beauty.

It's *pouring*.

I know I know, said Randeep. It just drips off straight onto my shoulders. Like from the roof into a rain bucket.

I can't hear you, said Jenny louder, what did you say?

I said fuck it.

I'm glad somebody said that.

Yes, said Randeep. I'm quite pleased it was me, too. Anyway, at least it's downhill this way.

I don't want to go on, said Charlie.

But you must, said Randeep, you can't stay here. We're

all going back now. Let's see how that little river is filling.

We may have to swim, said Cees to Charlie. Or I'll carry you over. I'll carry you all over. When you're old you will be able to say: that was the day a Dutchman carried me over the Kennet.

I'm game, said Shirley.

OK, said Charlie. I'll just walk down. Can I have the key to the car?

Don't drop it in the river, said Randeep. If you drop it in the river your name will be mud.

Mu-ud, said Debbie Inner Tube, mu-ud. I'm going to swoop and scoop.

Wenceslas and the children sped down the hill.

I can't walk fast, said Jenny.

We'll dry off, said Cees. I know a café.

You do? said Linda surprised.

I do.

A last pathway of baby blue crossed the sky to the far north, beyond Avebury and the next set of downs, beyond everywhere that might have belonged to this ancient network.

The first car door was opening and shutting as Beth with Jenny and David, his arm around her, were barely halfway down the hill. Linda was laughing and Cees smiling. Shirley Bates held on to Randeep to examine the heels on her impractical shoes while he looked up into the sky. Moth walked in a straight line, holding her jacket tight against her. Worrying at some discovery, Wenceslas ran back and forth at the trickling River Kennet. Shirley halted at a safe distance as Wenceslas shook himself. Randeep adjusted his turban, now much darker, and walked on.

LINNET

WIND RUSTLED THROUGH the willow. Lea felt the
boughs bending, watched the branches dip, heard
the leaves brushing other leaves. It was comfortable
enough lying in a fork of branches, lolling. Having the red
brick summer house in sight. Seeing the occasional sparkle
on the water. Looking downwards: the lilies, the glassy
pond belonging to the River Linnet. Away from the water,
where a few trees stood on rough turf, she could imagine
what had been there before: a garden. She recognised its
remnants: still the regal summer house with its cream-
painted doors, one door ajar. Still the garden walls, three
pocked but fiercely-red brick walls, the grassy ground.

When this tree moves the other trees move too,
branches sway and sway; angels carrying their messages;
the wind should be making ripples on the water but the
lilies won't allow it. Should she sing a song? For the
moment her fear has gone, her mind moved on from the
horse. Lolling is good—I feel so. Picking the trophies off my
young girl's chest. Crowflowers, daisies, columbines. This is
bindweed. It's poisonous to some animals, sometimes. It's
said the seeds contain *hallucinogenic* substances. It doesn't
smell. Who would have thought it would be growing at a
stately home. Though it grows under the ground for miles.
You can't forbid a plant to grow.

Terrible things happened in this garden that's no longer
here, my bones feel it. Still the trees will not settle after-
wards. Whispered conspiracies and confessions, silk clothes
parted. Or strollers out alone like me. Thinking they are

106

safe at last. Thinking *Ye mystic garden fold me close I love thee well.*

And then from nowhere: Come to me, come here—so the talk went. A quick dagger and a throat—*errant* lover's throat—is cut.

Or poison on a sword tip scratches home and starts its work: an anguished cry, a moan of fury blasts up to the sky. Pale looks and eyelids shutting, fainting and pain. The young and beautiful, dying.

Let the tree bend, the wind blow. The horse can't find its way here. The path is too narrow and the wooden bridge too flimsy. It can't pass through brick. It can stare at a gate or a door for as long as it likes, but it can't unbolt bolts, can't lift a latch.

Unless someone has tied a gay ribbon onto the latch and the horse pulls the ribbon with its teeth.

This is garden rue. Touch it and your skin will itch.

If anyone has to die at the hooves of a horse it should be Uncle Miroslaw. (He isn't my uncle really, he isn't *my* any-thing, he is mum's new friend.) I did well to avoid thinking his name for so long. To mention a name that should not be uttered means great misfortune. Too late. Utter no ummen-tionable names; cut your hair by the new moon. I long to push Uncle Miroslaw into a watery ditch, giving him pneu-monia, *splash!* Because it is on his account we have been going, weekend after weekend, to the houses and gardens. All so a man who is not an uncle, who is always *knowing* or *asking,* which somehow makes him annoying; all so a man who is not an uncle, with a smile that won't wipe off, dark wire for hair, could supposedly get to know our English life.

Smile, smile. He has been *revelling* in seeing an English

country house. The show bits on the lawn: the golden Suffolk punches, the sheepdog chasing ducks, the asthmatic old tractors that can't just stay in their sheds and die. Grinning. He grinned that you could call a horse a *punch* and a hedge be made of *box*. I'm so pleased to be at Ickworth, he said, this Georgian jewel. And turning to me with a strange look: *Didn't I tell you, you're never far from a horse.*

If I forget everything I cannot forget these words. Prophetic; as if he made the horse appear. Cats and dogs are never far, spiders and flies, but a horse? Those Suffolk horses were a warning. They may be golden with blonde tails you ache to touch but this doesn't tell how they really are. They are so *strong*. I just *shudder* when I think of one. Shudder shudder. Just as Uncle M was reading *These horses are looked after by prisoners* one of the minders went behind a horse and it kicked him so he fell in the dirt with his hand to his chest and had to be helped up. The biggest horses in England, he read — my uncle who isn't an *uncle*, whose crash course in Englishness we all crash away at every weekend, who mum says has enough energy for us all; who always has something to say, dark wire on his arms, who mum has called old blue eyes, who wherever we go always has a leaflet in his hand.

A hoof to his throat and by now Uncle Miroslaw would be lying flat on a plane back to Poland. Mum in black with a veil, sitting with her knees together by his coffin in the baggage hold.

What now? said mum after the Suffolk punches. I know: climb a tree by the pond with the lilies and observe mum and Uncle M and anyone who passes. I'm going back to that summer house, I said, I know exactly where it is and exactly the way back and I won't go anywhere else. I *know* they will come to check but they won't find me and so what. In the end we will be back together in the car, on our way home.

Perhaps Uncle Miroslaw will drive. Perhaps he will rub his eyes one time too many and forget which side of the road to drive on. One swerve and he could die in the River Linnet, live an English death with us all.

Sauntering towards the vanished garden, shaking my arms and hands about just for fun, passing the private church which is shut shut shut—and somehow still belongs to the faraway Marquis of Bristol—I was minding my own business when that great mottled horse with a rider in a black helmet galloped up from nowhere, out of the bowels of the Earth. It wasn't a punch; but huge. After stopping, it came straight towards me like a tank, faster than I could run. Wet my thumb, wipe it dry, cut my throat if I tell a lie—I was totally scared. The rider pulled and pulled to turn the horse away. It stood a few yards off, looking. It took no notice of other people walking. I was wearing white, I should have worn black. I had my hair tied, I should have left it loose. One shoe was unlaced, I should have had it tied. I should have touched my nose and toes.

The horse squared up ready.

My turn to die.

That horse was going to push me down and clunk its hoof into my chin so my neck snapped and I died all in one go.

I was so scared I opened my mouth and nothing came out. I spat three times on the ground and the rider somehow turned it aside again and rode off, the horse dropping its head and looking back. Now I will die later, or much later, depending if the horse returns. It will be wondering where I am. I feel it: It's looking for me.

I climbed a good old tree and lay in a big fork. I heard no hooves; one or two voices. Since no one came by I slid to the ground and went to pick some plants from the low hedges crisscrossing and arching, the *box* garden; so I had something to smell and to chew at. Mm, that must be sweet spinach, I was saying to myself. Mm, larkspur. Now maybe I'll fall sick and die. Then I went to the Linnet pond with the lilies and found the tree above the water. I lolled.

That one horse has changed all horses for me now. I loved that big horse on the hill at Uffington, which I *know* has a foal behind her, and when night comes they both step out of their chalk shapes, uncrook their stiff knees and shoulders, and amble down the hill to graze. Even mum thinks they do.

I picked at the daisies and columbines; one leaf, one petal at a time. The summer house has been there three centuries. They say a queen of Denmark sat there one afternoon. Uncle M was impressed by this. But he knows nothing of the knives and pistols and silk getting torn. As mum said: A queen has only to stop somewhere for a glass of water and it's history for ever.

Sure enough Uncle M and mum showed. They stopped almost below me. Don't worry, I heard him saying. But I am worrying, mum said, she's been so strange lately, talking to herself and *chanting*. It's just play, said Uncle Miroslaw, she's a girl; young girls live in their own world. As if you would know, said mum; but there's strange and strange. She walks about saying she's practising chore*ography* and won't say what she means, what's going on?

She's just a young girl, un-uncle Miroslaw said. He kissed mum. Uncle Miroslaw kissed mum. Speak of choreography: this doesn't fit the plan for today. He should be standing with her in the summer house, holding her hands for the last time. *Farewell, 'tis late and I must to Poland. War is war, who knows if I may return.* She falls back onto the lovely bench in despair, leaving the door ajar for centuries. The queen of Denmark goes by not noticing her weeping, asks for a glass of water and her visit is history for ever.

All I could see through the tree was his wire hair and a bit of mum's hair dyed too blondely and permed too curly; their hands had disappeared under their coats. I gripped a good branch and tried not to breathe. I saw one of my arms reflected in the pond.

Do you think she might be about the old church? said Uncle Miroslaw finally.

The gates are locked, said mum. But anything's worth trying.

Unsafe structure the notice read, said Uncle M being precise.

They made off at a fair pace but arm in arm. As if I would have gone there. As if I were mad. I shimmied further out on my branch careful not to lose my treasures.

The wind comes and goes; more angels' messages. The pond goes from dark to bright to dark again; the sun will be gone altogether soon.

The stems of bindweed always twine around objects counter clockwise. And pluck the petals and they resent it. The pink cups close. Drop it in the water—too late—and it may only spread further. There's fennel. My fingers itch. Is there an antidote. I feel drowsy. Is there an antidote to Uncle Miroslaw.

Maybe I should try another branch. No, no, methinks this one doth crack and would split in two.

That's a vole under the bank.

Pansies—for thoughts. First thought: dad the antidote to Uncle Miroslaw. Where is my dad. In another country. America.

Thought: It would take him a day to get here. He comes. Kills Uncle Miroslaw.

A grassy fragrance on my fingers.

Where has the vole gone?

Unsafe structure. I should move; watch I don't fall.

Back they come.

Miro she swore she would only take the one path so she must be here somewhere; it's getting late. The river is nice, he says. Yes the river, she says; but I don't like it here—it's a feeling I get. Feelings can deceive, says Uncle Miroslaw: they say the owl was a baker's daughter.

Never far from a horse.

What owl? says mum—you and your funny talk.

Kiss me, he says next. She hesitates before she goes ahead. *Slurp.* Why do they make me stretch so? Talking fainter and fainter. I wipe my own mouth; it's burning. Come here, he says, you've got something on you, what is this? It's a weed, says mum puzzled, it gets everywhere and now it's on me. They laugh. It's very hard, says mum—they snatch a kiss again—very hard. Hard? To get rid of, Miro. Anyway, says mum: since my daughter is not here, will you kiss me again?

Indeed, 'tis late. Is the horse locked up, the rider's helmet hanging from a peg? The wind rises, branches dip and wander. My eyes close; the last thing I see is sky.

TAGUS

They give us an imaginary map in the form of a city. A clock and a calendar, from which we cannot tell our age. They give us a hat so we can have our portraits made. They give us a ticket to heaven, which is nothing but a scene in a play. We have well brought-up ghosts in whose arms we can soundly sleep.

—NATÁLIA CORREIA

I HAVE A real map of a city I imagine, Lisbon. I don't go there; I just imagine going.

I go by train, I don't know why. In one of Europe's far corners, *Lisboa* makes for a long, tiring journey; the train with sleepers goes via Paris and Madrid, crossing France and Spain. I come into the Santa Apolónia station towards evening; a perfect point of arrival, on the edge of the Alfama district. Just steps from the hotel I shall be smelling the sardines and the basil and the coffee. Anticipation hurries me on, to the Hotel de Soares, though I somehow walk past it and have to go back. It has glass doors, and blue-and-white tiles decorating the space at the entrance.

My feet meet the carpet in steps which are suddenly heavy, tired, sapped of strength by the travel. I'm tired; but I'm here. I dump my rucksack beside the reception desk. The act of checking in, it's startling to discover, is done elbow to elbow with the hotel parrot; a creature which, with or without my awareness of it, has somehow always been here, noisy and fabulously red in a cage. It cocks its head as I write my name in an old-fashioned, oversized ledger. The end of its red-and-blue tail flicks the bars. When the formalities are completed it watches me bend down for my rucksack, dipping its head, and is still watching me as I glimpse it from the stairs. I think about it as I go to my room. If there was to be a bird I would have expected a pair, or at least a smaller bird, and a handsome green rather than red. Having such large parrots in cages is surely illegal. I have a room looking onto the street. There's a faint lavender smell. Again dropping my rucksack, I settle in quickly. I lean out of the window to washing hanging and satellite dishes and a moped spuming blue-grey fumes. *The city of the resigned poet and blue mosaics.*

You said that, Claire.

I hear music, guitars strumming. The street feels close, breathing next to me. Already I think I like it here. Checking the tap water is not brown, I decide to trust the whole of Lisbon and leave the contents of my rucksack strewn on the bed. I take to the hallway and think about the parrot; its life with the faded walls, dark carpeting and thick-spiced kitchen smells; how these are as familiar to it as they are strange and new to me. Then there I am, out there. The dusk of the evening warmly glows. A tram with painted silhouettes of children on the front clatters by, screeching, holding to the steep hill.

Yes, it's sunset. I settle in more with each step, and soon realise I have been walking, leisuredly and distracted, among couples, dogs and fireflies, down Rua da Alfândega towards the Tagus. The fireflies are there, but not visible. They will light their soft fires later, in mating by darkness. I know this from Claire.

I miss you. I don't accept there could be a good life without you.

I walk on. It's a beautiful autumn. The leaves on the trees have been performing, putting on that show of colour.

Yes, the sun has set. As Terreiro do Paço opens out before me, I can appreciate why this was once where coffee was laid out to dry. What a splendid place, Lisbon!—a city with the inviting quality of the human scale. Here in Lisbon, nonetheless—and rarely has anyone managed to part this city from the poet—lived Fernando Pessoa: *My happiest hours are those in which I think nothing, want nothing, when I do not even dream, but lose myself in some spurious vegetable torpor, moss growing on the surface of life.* I picture this wordsmith of almighty pessimism composing his Book of Disquiet. He wanders in a trance over the balustrades of a bridge; in mid-recital, overbalancing in a slow plunge, down into the waters of the Tagus, which he enters in hardly a splash.

Yet I know the Tagus is not like the Thames or the Seine. There are no such convenient bridges here. The river is virtually a sea, travelled by grain ships, container vessels and tugs, ferries crossing to the satellite conurbations of Seixal, Barreiro and Montijo. Nonetheless couples come to the waterfront. They seem to enjoy the promise of the future which is suggested by standing, as if posing, at the edge of a great stage, with this expanse of flat water for the auditorium floor, under a vast dome of sky.

After just six months Claire left, saying—out of the blue—her fiancé had been released from jail in France. Fiancé, jail, France? And—*ciao!*

The sunset is scattered with stray clouds. As I turn back from the water the last daylight reaches the doorway of a café, disappearing in its green watery light. A few bars of a *fado* seep out. Said Fernando Pessoa: *A mild unease slumbers in the false valleys of the streets.*

Claire and *Claude* were to meet in St Malo; from there to travel by motorbike to Lisbon.

Why did she tell me this? You and I had marriage

planned, she replied. Now Claude and I shall be doing it.

She stood there with a crash helmet, saying goodbye.

Doing what?

Our honeymoon, *mon chou et moi.*

My mouth dried; over and over the words ran through my head. Claire gripped the strap of the helmet held at her side. I felt lost, in a no-man's land.

Chou? Claude? What kind of a name is that?

Claude, she replied. Claude Hamon. 24, rue Barbet de Jouy. You're a fool.

Where did you get that helmet? I demanded.

I've always had it.

It's a motorbike helmet.

So? He has an English Norton motorbike.

What was he in jail for?

Drugs.

Drugs? What do you mean, drugs?

She shrugged.

Peddling drugs.

You're going on a honeymoon to Lisbon with a French convict on a motorbike? I'm stupefied. How is he going to pay for his part?

Pay? said Claire—who I can still picture as she was at that moment, licking the end of her sunglasses before sticking them high in her hair.

Did you say pay? What on earth do you mean? And what business is all this of yours? Why should I listen to all these questions? You want to know about money? What's got into you? Anyway I'll tell you. I can tell you we won't be sleeping in barns.

Since Claire told me about Claude, the motorbike, the fireflies waiting for them in the trees in Lisbon, I've done nothing but imagine them taking their honeymoon. Their totally exhausting, exhilarating, but romantic journey, the one overnight rest on the Santander ferry. Deep in sleep, the head of one buried in the other's shoulder blades, traversing the Bay of Biscay. Come morning, they roar first off the boat on his Norton machine. The Spanish sky is wide and blue, hot, even hotter than they might have liked. Two dark manes flowing from their crash helmets, keeping to the plains, they follow one of the old sheep trails, crossing the Portuguese border opposite the lovely Serra da Estrela. They power a route along the lakes at the foot of these mountains, enchanted by the countryside, by the thought of each other.

All this time I must have been staring at the café, attracted by the cool green light and maroon tablecloths. Another woman's voice, already another plaintive *fado*. I sat at a table outside. To fight fatigue I ordered coffee. Coffee, I said, *café con leche, sucré*.

The waiter nodded in a worldly way at this odd conglomerate of languages.

There is and was no way to test the authenticity of Claire's prison fiancé story. It sounds extraordinary. The truth can be extraordinary. The *El País* I found on the train seemed to be saying a fly got into the instrument panel of an airline jet and plunged two hundred and forty-seven people (and one fly) into the ocean. Must I discount something just because it sounds faintly preposterous?

I found myself turning to the map to see if I could walk from Terreiro do Paço to the tower of Belém. This landmark was so old it would have been seen by the ageing Vasco da Gama. There I could distract myself thinking of extraordinary sea journeys to India. How the tower was once a lighthouse out in the Tagus. The hotel brochure said people would be dancing to their ghetto-blasters under the turrets. I would strive not to think of Claire; her dancing, her golden skin and expensive bracelets. Not to remember being seduced by her. I had no idea seduction could be so direct, be as simple a matter as dancing close on a ragged carpet on a bland Sunday afternoon.

I caught a number 15 tram along the waterfront. Since I'm here, I told myself, I must soon go walking in the Estrela district. I like old buildings, worn stone, flaking façades; I want to feel its hills beneath my feet. The thought of the Estrela district, just the idea of possibly going there the next day, caused me to abandon a visit to the tower and get off the tram immediately. I stood at the kerbside, confused. I'm here, I thought, but not where I thought I would be. I was lost. Exposed as a foreigner, alone, making for a most uncomfortable feeling. Other than *fado, saudade*, I realised, I knew no Portuguese.

After a while everything Claire said left me guessing. She turned up at my doorstep to tell me she had just dined with a millionaire. He lived in a country house and owned a forest. She had left him that very hour, rejecting his advances to come to me at midnight. Had she really left a millionaire? I don't know; until the final moment I let everything pass unchallenged. She left little time for protest. Come here darling, she would say. I went where she said. I will show you the meaning of skin — her message ran — and perfume. I will now show you what a kiss may be, like this. Barely nineteen, walking naked; displaying brownness and confidence, hastening the invisible clamour for sex.

But now my body, the same body so readily aroused, has ordered me to lie down and sleep. Having snapped out of the familiar daydream of Claire and the millionaire (how many times had I recalled the doorstep, imagined her per-fume) and willing—hauling—myself back to the present, I walk not the way I came but back on a different route. The sight of the old rack-railway pulling up the steep Bairro Alto is a sudden draw, and I head for it. I squeeze into the next railcar that comes.

Out on the higher ground the air is damp. I feel water droplets on my cheeks like a cool powder. I face a mean-ingless building, a nondescript set of balconies stuck on a façade of vanilla. Across from it, shining pigeons infest the shining pavement next to a taxi-stand. I'm more lost than ever. A taxi has a door pressed back in invitation. I get in, say *Hotel de Soares* and point to its street on the map. In taking a taxi I would be getting there in comfort, I thought, and were it necessary I was ready to offer dollars not to face unwanted questions. I cannot say: yes this is my first visit, I'm here to forget my first love; I loved her because of the excitement. Just drive where I ask, I imagined myself saying. But we had already covered a good distance, and the driver left me to myself, tangled in the memory of an infat-uation.

At the hotel, the parrot has its eyes closed. My things are out where I left them. I sit on the bed, staring at the wash-basin; at a frame in flaky gold paint round the mirror. I move my things onto a chair. I lie down because this was my plan. I dream a little, a dream accompanied by the sight of pigeons. On waking I feel hungry. I get up, go downstairs and ask to see the dish of crab, *santola recheado*, having seen its picture in the hotel brochure. I think vaguely about the pigeons and exchange stares with the parrot, now biting morosely at the struts of its cage. The crab shown me looks the perfect replica of the creature in the brochure; this dis-turbs me for some reason. I apologise with sign language for not wanting to eat it. I am bid to sit alone at a big table, where I eat a rice pudding prepared with almonds.

In the deepening night the city stays quietly awake. I don't know why but I take another stroll down the Rua da Alfândega. The couples have thinned in number. The fireflies haven't come out after all. They aren't lighting up in the trees, aren't flitting at the far end of passageways; perhaps there are none. At the waterside the mist is turning to fog, into which the great span of the *Ponte 25 de Abril* at the river mouth has disappeared. City of pigeons and a scarlet parrot. Pigeons? I don't care for pigeons but, as I told Claire when things were at their height, when anything could be said without reproach: birds are the sacred animals, dinosaurs linking us to our furthest past. Screw them, she said, who wants dinosaurs around. She got up, walked about naked and sang a song on the guitar. She had no feeling for music but it was mesmerising the way she and the guitar made two golden tans. Naked too, I got evangelical about the birds and the dinosaurs. After all, I said, out of this past came the urge to make love. I was male and physical, and she wanted the male and physical. I wanted Claire.

Her honeymoon plan brought me here. But perhaps she never came at all; perhaps Claude is not a person but an idea, a desire, a means of exiting from the present. Perhaps. What will become of her? Of me? And where am I exactly? It's cold; a thick chill clamours, tries to sit round my throat. Why had I come out again; I should have packed a scarf, come better prepared, have packed more clothes altogether.

I can see little: visibility is closing. In the hidden pathways of the streets a tram clangs louder. With great effort I haul myself out of the trance into which I have sunk and, like a dog, shake off the dank darkness of the fog. But the fog stays. Its very thickness hides everything beyond an arm's length. The tram stops. I keep waiting for it to start again, but it doesn't. All the traffic seems to have stopped. There is a quiet now in this city. Pressed in by the fog, I walk. To retrace my route my only guide is the line of the kerb.

When nothing else is left visible, I fold the map, cross the room, and put it back into the drawer.

ACKNOWLEDGEMENTS

I WOULD LIKE to thank the editors of the publications in which several of these stories first appeared. 'Elbe' was published in *The Yellow Nib* (Seamus Heaney Centre), 'Seine' and 'Butley' in *Stand*, 'Stour' in *Northwords Now*, 'Linnet' in *Staple* and 'Tagus', under its original title 'Sunset', in *Ambit*. Black Dog Books kindly gave permission for Ronald Blythe to be quoted from his book *Field Work*.

I would also very much like to thank Thor Müller for his splendid guidance; Robin Robertson, for his generous assistance with 'Blyth'; and again my most excellent reader, Stella Chapman.